# "I Have A Picnic In The Car,"

Connor whispered, as if confiding a great secret. "Not just your ordinary picnic either...it's a *chocolate* picnic."

"I've never had one of those before," Maxie gasped. She was becoming weak all over from the achingly pleasurable sensation of his breath stirring in her ear.

"I'm taking you away from your ranch, your garden and your cows," Connor told her, rubbing his nose lightly against the baby-soft skin of her neck. "You haven't lived until you've had a chocolate picnic."

"Have you?"

"Lived?"

"Had a chocolate picnic?"

"No." He kissed her forehead lightly, then forced himself to step back from her. Her incredible eyes never lost their spellbinding appeal. "I guess that means I've never lived before today, either."

Dear Reader,

As we celebrate Silhouette's 20th anniversary year as a romance publisher, we invite you to welcome in the fall season with our latest six powerful, passionate, provocative love stories from Silhouette Desire!

In September's MAN OF THE MONTH, fabulous Peggy Moreland offers a *Slow Waltz Across Texas.* In order to win his wife back, a rugged Texas cowboy must learn to let love into his heart. Popular author Jennifer Greene delivers a special treat for you with *Rock Solid,* which is part of the highly sensual Desire promotion, BODY & SOUL.

Maureen Child's exciting miniseries, BACHELOR BATTALION, continues with *The Next Santini Bride,* a responsible single mom who cuts loose with a handsome Marine. The next installment of the provocative Desire miniseries FORTUNE'S CHILDREN: THE GROOMS is *Mail-Order Cinderella* by Kathryn Jensen, in which a plain-Jane librarian seeks a husband through a matchmaking service and winds up with a Fortune! Ryanne Corey returns to Desire with a *Lady with a Past,* whose true love woos her with a chocolate picnic. And a nurse loses her virginity to a doctor in a night of passion, only to find out the next day that her lover is her new boss, in *Doctor for Keeps* by Kristi Gold.

Be sure to indulge yourself this autumn by reading all six of these tantalizing titles from Silhouette Desire!

Enjoy!

*Joan Marlow Golan*

Joan Marlow Golan
Senior Editor, Silhouette Desire

Please address questions and book requests to:
Silhouette Reader Service
U.S.: 3010 Walden Ave., P.O. Box 1325, Buffalo, NY 14269
Canadian: P.O. Box 609, Fort Erie, Ont. L2A 5X3

# Lady with a Past
## Ryanne Corey

Published by Silhouette Books
**America's Publisher of Contemporary Romance**

For the star that watched over me
and the man who waited.

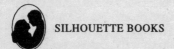 SILHOUETTE BOOKS

ISBN 0-373-76319-0

LADY WITH A PAST

This edition published by arrangement with Harlequin Books S.A.

® and TM are trademarks of Harlequin Books S.A., used under license.
Trademarks indicated with ® are registered in the United States Patent
and Trademark Office, the Canadian Trade Marks Office and in other
countries.

Visit Silhouette at www.eHarlequin.com

**Printed in U.S.A.**

**Books by Ryanne Corey**

Silhouette Desire

*The Valentine Street Hustle* #615
*Leather and Lace* #657
*The Stranger* #764
*When She Was Bad* #950
*Lady with a Past* #1319

---

## RYANNE COREY

An author of bestselling romance novels, Ryanne Corey lives in Idaho in the shadow of the Teton Mountains, "the best place in the world to write and write and write." She has written over twenty novels and is recognized for the true-to-life humor and sensuality of her characters. She has received several awards over the last few years, including *Romantic Times Magazine*'s Lifetime Achievement Award and award for Best Series Novel. She has long believed that life is too serious to be taken too seriously. In her writing she enjoys creating appealing and amusing characters that take their first breath on page one, endearing themselves to the readers long after the book is finished. "For me," Ryanne says, "bringing a smile to someone's face is what life is all about."

Nothing is more satisfying to her than hearing from readers who share her enjoyment of "love and laughter." You can write to her at P.O. Box 328, Tetonia, ID 83452. Please include a SASE if a reply is desired.

# IT'S OUR 20th ANNIVERSARY!
## We'll be celebrating all year,
## Continuing with these fabulous titles,
## On sale in September 2000.

# One

Connor Garrett was the first to admit he enthusiastically spoiled himself. He liked his little creature comforts, enjoyed his no-limit credit cards, sent all his clothes, including his undershorts, out to be cleaned and had magnificent houses on both coasts. He couldn't make peace with his microwave, but that hardly mattered since his housekeepers—one capable gray-haired lady per house—handled the cooking on the few occasions he actually ate in. In fact, with the exception of the mysterious microwave oven, he couldn't think of a time in recent memory when he'd come up against anything that had disrupted his cheerful existence.

Until now.

First of all, his six-foot-plus frame was folded into a very irritating rental car. He was too tall for the sporty little number that had looked so appealing at the Jackson Hole airport. This necessitated him driving with the sunroof open, which would have solved the problem nicely…if it hadn't started to rain. His dark, golden-brown hair was well on its way from damp to drenched.

He'd also discovered the terrible habit Wyoming's wild animals had of using the highways as their own private crosswalks. Since leaving the airport he'd seen elk, moose and a terrifying number of skunks strolling down the center line. This was not the way things were done in Los Angeles, and the only wild animals that frequented New York streets were taxi drivers.

Still, Connor's black mood had less to do with the driving conditions than it did with a certain woman the world knew only as Glitter Baby. Connor was looking for her and had been for the past ten days. She didn't want to be found. So far, she was winning.

He glanced down at the rain-spotted photograph on the seat beside him. It was a haunting picture, a full-length shot of a reed-thin woman with heavily shadowed violet eyes and cascades of glorious, golden-blond hair. Her skin was pale, almost luminescent; it was hard to tell where she ended and her sheer ivory dress began. Her wide lips shimmered wetly with cinnamon gloss, sulky and shaped for sin. For a time, hers had been the most famous face in America.

"Where the hell did you disappear to, lady?" Connor muttered. "How could someone with a face like yours disappear without a trace?"

He turned his attention back to the road just in time to avoid flattening yet another slow-moving skunk. Connor was tired of traveling constantly. He was tired of staying in motels with names like Fairly Reliable Bob's. He particularly disliked hopping on tiny little tinfoil airplanes to fly over great big mountains. He had a sinking feeling he was on a wild-goose chase, but he refused to give up. That would be admitting defeat, and in this particular circumstance, Connor couldn't afford to fail.

The mobile phone in his jacket pocket rang, and he fished it out, keeping a wary eye on the road. Only one person had this particular number, his assistant Morris Gold. "Speak to me, Morris. Any luck in Texas? I know it's a big place…no, I don't want to interview Alan Greenspan for the show. Who wants to hear about interest rates for sixty minutes? I told you before, this interview is for sweeps week and it has to be something special. No one has been able to find this lady for two years. It'll be a real coup if Public Eye is the first." There was a short silence, broken only by the sound of raindrops hitting the leather upholstery. "No, I'm not trying to be difficult. I have a damn good reason for going to all this trouble, but you don't need to know it. What do you mean, you're starting to dream about her? No, you can't fall in love with a picture. I'm an expert at not falling in love, Morris—I know these things. You're losing your focus. Call me if anything turns up, all right?"

Connor tossed the phone down on the seat with a weary sigh. He had worked as a highly successful television journalist for over six years now, but had never come up against a challenge quite like this. Glitter Baby had dominated the fickle world of high fashion for nearly eight years. Even at the age of fourteen, when she had first begun modeling, she had radiated a powerful combination of innocence and sexuality that left women envious and men gasping for air. When she had abruptly retired two years ago at the venerable age of twenty-two, there had been no announcement of future plans. Even with Connor's research staff scrambling in all directions, there was scant information available on who the woman really was, why she had vanished or where she might have gone. She had been born Frances Calhoon in Redfern, Wyoming, and her father had farmed there until his death six years earlier. Her mother had moved away since, although none of their former neighbors in Redfern knew where. End of story. Connor had an infallible sense of what the public hungered for, and the true story behind the disappearing supermodel had the makings of a dynamite show…not to mention the fact he had a promise to keep.

But first he had to find her.

Every lead his office could come up with was being investigated. Someone claimed to have seen her at a health club in Palm Beach. Another tip claimed she had gained 150 pounds and joined a nunnery, while yet another maintained she had opened her own tattoo parlor in the Philippines. Connor himself was following up on a tip that she had recently been seen at a cattle-judging competition at the Western Wyoming State Fair. He was dogged, if not particularly hopeful. Cows and supermodels did not compute.

Again and again he found himself sneaking sideways glances at her photograph. The camera adored her; he could understand why she had achieved such astonishing notoriety. Unlike the vacuous gazes of

other ennui-drenched models, her eyes shone wetly
with fire and fantasy. Part waif, part siren, and the
combination was a powerful commercial aphrodisiac.

He wondered what it would be like to hold her.

After a restless night at the small motel in Oakley,
Wyoming, Connor again went through his routine of
visiting shops and cafés, showing Frances Calhoon's
picture and hearing the same comments over and
over: "Of course I know who she is. I've never seen
her around here, though." Then, if Connor happened
to be talking to a member of the male sex over the
age of thirteen: "I wish I had."

Somewhat of a celebrity in his own right, Connor
wore his usual semi-disguise of sunglasses and a
baseball cap pulled low over his choppy mane of
golden-brown hair. Unrecognized, he followed the
western-style boardwalk up one side of the main
street and down the other. He was oblivious to the
female eyes that followed his rolling, somewhat
cocky gait, lingering wistfully on his broad shoulders
and snug-fitting faded jeans. Since his college days
as a football star, women had enthusiastically appreciated Connor's golden-boy good looks and he liked
to think he did his part by appreciating them right
back. When a knee injury had derailed his promising
professional football career and left him in career
limbo, he had crossed his fingers and accepted a job
offer from his godfather, Jacob Stephens, the head
honcho at a television cable network. Jacob had assured him that he had the presence to hold his own
while interviewing celebrities, athletes and anyone
else who was making news.

Connor discovered the job was far less stressful

physically and mentally than football had ever been. What it boiled down to basically was flirting with pretty women, trading war stories with egotistical men and asking whatever question came to mind. Connor felt a little guilty about the generous salary he was making, since he never actually broke a sweat, but the powers that be seemed enormously pleased with his "work."

Truth be told, Connor was amazed at his own success. He knew his looks and manner were not quite the norm for a television journalist. Where others were suitably somber, he was boyishly spirited. Where others were spritzed and polished to perfection before air time, Connor threatened the life of any makeup artist who approached him with a powder puff or a can of hairspray. Still, Public Eye managed to consistently top the ratings, which Connor modestly attributed to the luck of the Irish. Female members of the viewing audience, however, attributed its popularity to his longish, beautifully dishevelled hair, heavy-lidded amber eyes and a look so sweet you could pour it on a waffle. In fact, Morris liked to razz Connor by referring to him as "eye candy." Actually, Connor didn't enjoy the emphasis put on his looks, but he was basically an easygoing fellow who didn't like to make waves. Consequently, he collected his paycheck twice a month and resigned himself to enjoying the ride while it lasted. If he was occasionally bored, he told himself all men who couldn't play football for a living were probably bored. Then he went over his financial portfolio and felt much better.

Still, this particular assignment was something out of the ordinary and a far cry from boring. Normally,

Connor would have been content to let his staff and field investigators do the footwork, but time was growing short and none of his leads so far had panned out. This had become a challenge, and the former quarterback often found himself yearning for a challenge—not to mention the fact he owed Jacob Stephens a tremendous debt of gratitude for seeing him through a difficult time in his life. Jacob had long been making plans to buy out a struggling network, and ruling the ratings during sweeps week would put the icing on a lucrative acquisition. Connor owed his godfather that much, and a great deal more.

When he came to an establishment called Howdy-Do Farm & Feed, he rolled his eyes and nearly passed by it. Then he recalled the cattle-judging competition, sighed and tugged his ball cap further down on his head. More than likely he was going to make a damn fool of himself. In his experience, celebrities did not hang out in feed stores.

It was a bustling day at the Howdy-Do, probably because of the fertilizer sale advertised on a sign at the checkout counter. For the most part, shoppers appeared to be of the middle-aged, bow-legged and leathery variety. The aroma of fertilizer hung heavily in the air.

Connor pulled off his sunglasses and, holding up Glitter Baby's photograph, approached the teenage clerk at the checkout. The young fellow's jaw dropped like a hinge had broken.

"Sorry to interrupt you." Connor smiled. "I'm looking for someone. Have you seen this woman around town?"

"I'm looking for her, too," the boy mumbled,

eyes stretched to a breaking point. "Have been all
my life. Hot damn...why can't someone like that
come into this store, that's what I'd like to know?
Man, around here, it's the same girls over and over,
the ones you go to school with, the ones you see at
church—"

"Sounds like a bummer," Connor interrupted,
rubbing a weary hand over his eyes. "I take it you
haven't seen her, then?"

"*Believe* me," the clerk said earnestly, "I would
know if she'd ever been in Oakley. She's that model,
right? Spice Baby or somethin'?"

"Glitter Baby," Connor corrected, tugging the
photograph out of the boy's clinging fingers.
"Thanks anyway, pal."

"If you want I could tape her picture up and ask
folks—"

"That's not necessary," Connor said. "Do you
know which road I take to get to Riverside?"

"Highway 33 east," the boy replied, somewhat
crestfallen. "Take a right at the next stop sign and
you're on your way. Hey, you don't happen to have
an extra picture, do you? I'd give anything to have
one for my bedroom."

"No," Connor snapped, finding this teenager and
his raging hormones a little irritating. He turned on
his heel, colliding chest to chest with a shopper who
had just come up behind him. A light bulb went on
in Connor's brain: *generous breasts, very female.*
The luck of the Irish strikes again.

"My fault," the woman apologized, bending over
to scoop up her cowboy hat that had fallen on the
floor. She wore jeans, a denim shirt and dusty boots,
apparently the official uniform of Wyoming. Her

glossy chestnut hair was pulled back into a swinging ponytail, her eyes shaded by a silky fringe of bangs across her forehead. Connor thought the wide smile she gave him was fresh and quite charming. Her figure was full and luscious; even a heavy work shirt couldn't disguise her generous womanly curves. No wonder farmers' daughters had a reputation for being quite fetching in a milk-and-honey sort of way.

He grinned and shook his head, white teeth flashing in his California-tan face. "No, it was absolutely my fault. Are you all right?"

She laughed, low and throaty, fitting the cowboy hat firmly on her head. "I'm hardy. I'll survive."

"Well, as long as I've got your attention…" Connor held out his photograph, noticing that the edges were becoming dog-eared. "I'm looking for this woman. Do you remember ever seeing her around town?"

"She's famous, Maxie," the clerk put in, shamelessly eavesdropping. "Remember that model who disappeared a couple of years ago? That's her."

The woman studied the picture for several seconds, then scratched her sunburned nose and shrugged. "Sorry I can't help you. I'll tell you," she added, her voice tinged with the lilting western twang Connor was becoming familiar with, "someone like that wouldn't go unnoticed for long in this town. Robby, I need three bags of fertilizer. Put it on my account and I'll pull the truck around back to load it."

Connor touched her elbow as she turned to walk away. "You're sure? Someone thought they saw her at the tri-county fair last month."

"Everybody goes to the fair," she replied dismissively. "I was there, and I didn't see any famous faces in the crowds."

"Miss Rodeo Wyoming was there," Robby said hopefully, as if offering a substitute. "I saw her...she was real pretty."

"If I was looking for Miss Rodeo Wyoming," Connor replied flatly, "that news would make me the happiest of men."

The young woman chuckled on her way out the door. "I don't hold out much hope for you, buddy, but good luck just the same. See you 'round the back, Robby."

The muscles in Connor's shoulders were bunched with tension. He was tired. He was frustrated. Somewhere in the background he could hear Robby offer him five bucks for Glitter Baby's picture. Connor advised him to get a life and walked out into the parking lot. It looked like rain again, and the wind was picking up. He was so discouraged he was seriously considering calling Morris and telling him to track down Alan Greenspan. Lord knew he would be easier to find than one Frances Calhoon.

A dusty white pickup pulled out of the parking lot, tires spitting gravel. The brunette named Maxie, Connor thought absently, was in a hurry. She must be looking forward to getting that fertilizer home and doing whatever it was country people did with fertilizer.

Except...

Connor's flesh started prickling, from his toes to his scalp. A dawning realization kicked his heart into double time. *Except* Maxie hadn't driven around the back to load her fertilizer. She had sped out of the parking lot as if all the hounds in hell were after her.

Connor sat down abruptly, right there on the front steps of the store. His mind was spinning. He brought Glitter Baby's picture out of his jacket pocket and stared with fierce concentration. The chin, that stubborn chin was less angular in Maxie's face, but still similar. They were both of the same height. Frances Calhoon was a blonde and Maxie a brunette, but that meant nothing. The sultry waif in the photograph looked to be little more than a hundred pounds. Maxie had filled out her jeans with a mature woman's figure. Still....

Connor had another memory, an echo of something only his subconscious had registered at the time. He recalled seeing a split-second flash of Maxie's eyes before she'd replaced her hat, his subconscious noting an unusual color. Not brown, not hazel...

*Violet.* Glitter Baby's trademark, soul-stabbing violet eyes that rendered even the most jaded arbiters of beauty completely smitten. Connor had studied a hundred photographs, screened hours of videotapes. He knew her eyes better than his own, was intensely familiar with every mood, every subtle, sensual nuance they could project. He was no more immune to her powerful charisma than any other red-blooded man. One look from her eyes and the world stopped, shifted, and began spinning in a new orbit.

Maxie had those eyes.

"Hot damn," he whispered, the ghost of a smile touching his mouth.


Busted.

The important thing was not to panic. She panicked anyway. Frances Maxine Calhoon paced her front porch from one end to the other and back again, wringing her hands and whimpering. Her dog Boo, an enormous black lab who preferred naps to exercise, waddled loyally behind, now and then offering sympathetic whining and struggling for air. Boo had never seen his owner in a state of extreme agitation. Maxie hadn't been in a state of extreme agitation for two years. It had been blissful, wonderful, healing, therapeutic...and she was terrified it was over.

This little ranch in the middle of Nowhere, Wyoming, had been her refuge, her heaven-sent second chance. She knew without a shadow of a doubt it had saved her life. Two years ago she had weighed ninety seven pounds, smoked incessantly and slept less than an hour or two a night. She had debilitating migraines, her hands shook dreadfully and she neglected to eat for days at a time. Her agent sent her to a series of doctors who prescribed sleeping pills, tranquilizers and anti-depressants. Her trainer advised colon-cleansing, aromatherapies and a nicotine patch. Her friends borrowed her clothes and her pills and her money and always made sure they were standing next to her when tabloid photographers closed in for yet another shot. After eight years in the glare of the spotlight, Maxie was spent, coming apart at the seams, and no one seemed to realize or care how close she was to a complete breakdown. It was almost too late before she realized the creation known as Glitter Baby was first, last and always a stepping stone for others' interests. If she was to survive, she had to save herself.

She had been twenty-two-years old.

At the time, her widowed mother had started a new life in Oakley, Wyoming, running an antique shop in the nondescript little town. It was the perfect place for the runaway supermodel to start over, to learn to breathe and sleep and hope again. She retired without warning, used her savings to buy out her endorsement contracts and disappeared without a trace. She'd exchanged her first name for her middle name and become Maxie Calhoon. She had never looked back.

Until today. She hadn't realized the stranger in the feed store was Connor Garrett of television fame until he had spoken directly to her. She knew at that instant, even before she had looked at Glitter Baby's photograph, that the jig was up. This man was from the world she used to inhabit, a world she knew only too well. If he could benefit from publicizing her whereabouts, he would.

She became conscious of poor Boo's exhausted wheezing and stopped her frenzied pacing. Sweet dog, he had no idea the sky was falling in on them. He only knew he'd missed his mid-morning nap and his mistress had suddenly gone crazy. Maxie sat on the porch swing and scratched Boo under the chin until his big brown eyes began to droop. "That's it, sweetheart," she whispered. "Go to sleep and dream about big fat kitty cats…that's right, lie down."

Boo was asthmatic, overweight and incurably lazy, but he was her first true friend. She had confided in him all the regrets and mistakes of the past, and together they had celebrated her little accomplishments, such as learning to eat without guilt. Boo was a very good listener and fine company, particularly if she shared her SpaghettiOs with him. He didn't know or care who she had been in her previous life.

Heaven help her, she didn't want to lose it all now.

Connor Garrett could so easily put an end to her peaceful exile. Maxie wasn't at all sure she had fooled him with her careless indifference, either. There had been something in his dark eyes when he looked at her, a burning intensity that contrasted with his boyish baseball cap and casual L.A. Lakers sweatshirt. Sooner or later he was bound to put one and one together. For Maxie, that would mean the beginning of the end.

She gazed out at her sunwashed pasture, her eyes growing misty as she watched the newest addition to her fledgling herd of Holsteins frolic through the dandelions. Glitter Baby, that naughty darling of the high-fashion set, was raising cows. She fed them, milked them and read endless books about them. Granted, her new career put her in a much lower tax bracket than when she'd been modeling. *Much*, much lower. Fortunately, it looked like her struggling hand-to-mouth operation was going to get a desperately needed shot in the arm. While in town, she'd stopped by the bank and filled out papers for a loan that would see her through the coming winter. If it was approved, she would be home-free.

Still, should the truth about Glitter Baby's new occupation get out, the tabloids would have an absolute field day. For the first time in a long, long while Maxie found herself worrying about what people would say. *Did anyone test her DNA to positively identify her? Have you seen the mud-colored thing she did with her hair? And the weight she's put on…talk about heifers….*

Maxie stopped herself, putting a chokehold on her negative thoughts. She was letting her imagination run wild, imagining consequences that might never happen at all. She closed her eyes and took a deep, fortifying breath. What other people thought of her was no longer a concern, vital to neither her professional nor her private life. These days Maxie Calhoon pleased herself, and by doing so, had finally begun to build a healthy self-esteem. She wouldn't allow herself to go backward, not when she'd worked so hard and come so far. It could very well be that Connor Garrett had no idea who she was, would never dream of connecting Glitter Baby with Maxie at the feed store. Heaven knew the two women had nothing whatsoever in common...though they were one and the same.

*What a tangled web we weave,* Maxie thought, rubbing her throbbing temples. All she could do was hope and pray for the best. Maybe someday she would think back to that morning in the feed store when she had come face-to-face with her past and smile at her own paranoia. And maybe someday her cows would sprout wings and fly.

She would go inside, heat up a bowl of SpaghettiOs, make some peanut-butter toast and have a nice lunch. Then she had chores to do. The lawn needed to be cut and the vegetable garden needed to be fertilized and turned under....

Damn. No fertilizer.

For a man she had never actually met, Connor Garrett was doing an excellent job of ruining her entire day.

# Two

Could it be the wrong address?

Connor got out of his car and took off his sunglasses, blinking at the modest log cabin set a half mile back from the main road. Granted, it had a *Little House on the Prairie* kind of appeal—each of the windows had flower boxes crowded with cheerful yellow blooms, the front yard was nicely kept and a thick row of pine trees edged the gravel driveway. A wooded creek cut through the front of the property at an angle, sparkling in the sunset like so many diamonds flowing by. Beyond the house was a weathered red barn and a small pasture where several cows grazed.

It was a nice enough setting, but hardly the sort of place he would have imagined a woman like Glitter Baby would choose as home. Connor had done his homework on his mercurial subject. He knew she had owned luxury apartments both in America and abroad, but never had the time or interest to fully furnish any of them. She seldom stayed in any one place for more than a week at a time, and had often professed herself to feel most at home in four-star hotels.

Still, perhaps this unassuming ranch house was Glitter Baby's way of hiding in plain sight. Robby at the feed store had given Connor very clear directions to Maxie's place. It hadn't been at all difficult obtaining the information; Connor had traded his photograph of Glitter Baby for the address. Fortunately, he had a portfolio of over 200 pictures in his rental car, along with files of dozens of interviews from magazines. He felt he could spare one to enrich Robby's fantasy life and further his own research.

He returned to his car and coasted slowly down the gravel drive, preferring not to give advance notice of his arrival. The white truck parked in the shade of an aspen tree told him she was home. He didn't want her bolting out the back before he had a chance to talk to her.

He was surprised at his quietly labored breathing and the erratic rhythm of his heart. He had never found himself quite so fascinated with any of his subjects as he was now. Knowing that he was so affected was unnerving, particularly for a man who had survived repeated sackings by humongous homicidal defensive linemen.

Connor actually had no idea what he would say when he saw her. He didn't know what to expect, so at this point, he was taking things one step at a time. He couldn't stop thinking that whatever the next few minutes held for him, good or bad, they would be different from anything he'd ever experienced before.

In the past two years, Maxie had become an avid fan of sunsets. She never missed one if she could help it; possibly because she couldn't recall actually taking the time to enjoy a sunset in all the years she had modeled. Fluorescent lights had surrounded her day and night, artificial, hot and dry. Photographer's lights, neon lights in smoke-filled clubs and incessant flashing lights from the ever-present press. Bright, empty and blinding.

But a good sunset...now *there* was true magic, and something she had never appreciated until moving back to Wyoming. Perched on the top rail of the corral, Maxie studied the world slipping into night with a dreamy intensity. She knew how quickly a brilliant watercolor sunset faded to the comforting blue shadows of night. No two sunsets were alike, but each was a work of art in its own way. How lovely it would be, she thought wistfully, if the world looked at people the same way, knowing each was different and wonderfully unique. Maxie's eyes had been acclaimed, her cheekbones envied, her haircut widely imitated. And yet, when all was said and done, she had realized, the world knew nothing about her at all. How could they? Maxie had known so little about herself at that point.

She wondered how long it would be before people like Connor Garrett realized Glitter Baby no longer existed. Her demise was the best thing that had ever happened to Maxie Calhoon. No longer was she the neurotic woman who cried over a broken nail or insisted on weighing herself three times a day. These days she couldn't care less what the scales told her she weighed. Ah, and best of all, food had taken its rightful and revered place in her life, from SpaghettiOs to Lucky Charms to crackers and milk in bed. She ate. She slept. She worked with her hands and her mind and her heart. This journey of finding out who she was was turning out to be the most satisfying trip of her life. Why did that damned Connor Garrett want to ruin it all? Didn't he have anything better to do than make life miserable for a humble dairy farmer?

She heard footsteps on the gravel, looked over her shoulder and realized she could ask him herself.

He was walking towards the corral in a crimson haze of late-afternoon sunlight. His hands were tucked into the pockets of his jeans and his sneakers kicked up little clouds of dust as he walked. Creating disturbances, it seemed, came naturally to Connor Garrett. The baseball cap was missing and his longish golden-brown hair moved over his forehead with the restless evening breeze. His head was tilted quizzically as he approached, his bright-eyed gaze never leaving her face. And Boo, that traitorous canine, was bobbing along beside him like a drooling, furry welcome committee.

No place to hide, Maxie thought miserably. Which left her no alternative but to bluff. She climbed off the fence, slapping her palms clean on her jeans. "Well, this here's a surprise," she drawled. "I didn't expect to see you again. You lost, or somethin'?"

"Save the country-girl accent," Connor suggested. "It's overdone, anyway. You forgot your fertilizer, *Maxie*. Young Robby at the feed store gave

me your address, so I thought I'd bring it out to you.
I put it on your porch.''

"Such a good Samaritan." Maxie forced a tight
smile. "And what did you give young Robby in
exchange for my address?"

"A picture," he said softly, "of you."

In truth, Connor thought it a miracle he could
make any sound at all. He'd stood face-to-face with
any number of celebrities, had wined and dined them
and cheerfully pushed the necessary buttons to get a
good story. This was different. Connor couldn't quite
get away from the fact that he was a fully functioning
male and she was…hell, she was *Glitter Baby*.

Two years, he realized, had changed her in remarkable ways…and yet not at all. Her eyes, completely free of makeup, were intensely violet against
her sun-browned skin. Her shoulder-length hair,
glossy brown with deep auburn highlights, had been
freed from its ponytail and washed over her shoulders in no particular style. The impossibly generous
shape of her dusky rose lips had inspired many a
male fantasy, an understandable reaction. Connor
was somewhat inspired himself at the moment. How
on earth had this unforgettable lady escaped recog-
nition? Was everyone in this town blind?

Maxie watched him with the cool composure of
one who was used to being the focus of attention.
"Your mother should have taught you better manners. It's rude to stare."

"My mother was a politician's wife. She paid people to stare at her. It made her very happy. Besides,
it couldn't bother you too much. You spent eight
extremely profitable years being stared at."

"I can't imagine what you're talking about."

Connor grinned, admiring her pluck. "You know damn well what I'm talking about."

"You poor confused man. Do you have a short-term memory problem? How old are you, forty-five or so? That's quite young to be going senile."

"Thirty-four," Connor corrected. "And I still have all my own teeth, too."

Maxie shrugged. "You look much older in person than on television."

"You know who I am?" Pleased, he crossed his arms over his broad chest and began rocking back and forth on the heels of his sneakers. "I'm flattered. Why didn't you say something when I met you at the feed store?"

"I said I knew who you were, Mr. Garrett," Maxie retorted. "I didn't say I was a fan. Thank you for delivering my fertilizer. Having said that, I'm now going to walk you to your car and wave enthusiastically while you drive away."

"I'm beginning to feel unwanted." Connor lagged behind as she marched towards the house, a blissful smile on his face as he thoroughly appreciated the indignant rhythm of her rounded derriere. "We need to talk. Can't you spare me a minute? I promise, it could be well worth your while."

"*My* mother told me never to talk to strangers. You're very strange, therefore I don't want to talk to you."

"Now who's being rude? I've done nothing to—" He gave a low whistle. "Will you look at that? Holy cow…!"

Ever mindful of her Holsteins' health, Maxie stopped and looked back. Connor Garrett was down on his haunches in front of the vegetable garden in the side yard. Boo had crouched down likewise, his head tilted inquisitively. "*What* are you doing?" she demanded, her patience wearing thin.

He looked up at her, his finger jabbing in the direction of the cabbages. "I just saw a rabbit."

"And your point is?"

"It had *bent ears*," Connor stressed. "Like they were broken or something. I swear, it was the weirdest thing I've ever seen. He just ducked under the cabbages."

Maxine rolled her eyes. "His ears are supposed to look like that. That's Harvey. He's a lop-eared rabbit. He lives in the garden and helps me eat the produce. You don't get out to the country much, do you?"

Connor stood up, a wave of color rising in his face. "Hey, very few of my acquaintances keep rabbits as pets, bent-eared or otherwise. When I saw him, I thought the poor guy was crippled or something. Why the name Harvey?"

"I'm a big Jimmy Stewart fan."

"So why didn't you name it Jimmy Stewart?"

"Didn't you ever see the play *Harvey?* Or the movie? Jimmy Stewart had this imaginary rabbit—" She broke off abruptly. Connor Garrett was the enemy, and it wouldn't be smart to strike up any sort of friendship. "Never mind, Mr. Garrett. I'm sure you have better things to do than talk about my rabbit."

"Not really. Why won't you call me Connor?"

She gave him a killer smile, a weapon left over from her life in the fast lane. "I treat all people of your advanced age with respect, Mr. Garrett. Let's get moving. It's getting cold out here and you're keeping me from my dinner."

Connor dropped in behind her again, making a soft "meow" sound deep in his throat. She glared at him over her shoulder, but kept walking. Connor's low-slung canary-yellow rental car looked quite ridiculous next to her rugged power-wagon. It also appeared…locked. With the keys in the ignition.

"Are you *kidding* me?" Maxie walked around the car, trying both doors. "What kind of idiot locks his keys in the car?"

"I resent that," Connor said in an injured tone. "Are you implying I did it on purpose? You have a definite ego problem if you think I want your story that bad."

"What about the sunroof? Maybe we could slide it—"

Connor tried to look suitably mournful. It was difficult, considering he was enjoying himself enormously. "The sunroof doesn't work. It's broken. I plan on giving that rental company a piece of my mind when I return the car. I was assured this car was in perfect working—"

"Oh, shut up." She stared at him, murder in her violet eyes. "You probably worked this whole thing out in advance. Locked the keys in the car, glued the sunroof closed—"

"I'm not even going to dignify that with an answer. Besides, you told me to shut up." Connor tried both doors himself, grunting as if exerting great effort. "Well, this *is* a stroke of poor luck."

"Luck has nothing to do with it."

"I'll have to call a locksmith. Do you mind if I use your phone?"

Maxie was getting a migraine, her first in two years. "I'll tell you something, Garrett. Even if I *was* your missing model, which I'm not, I would never, ever, *ever* consent to an interview with a sneaky, opportunistic, underhanded, oily—''

"Oily?" Sneaky, opportunistic and underhanded Connor could live with. Oily was a slur on his personal hygiene. "That was below the belt, Ms. Calhoon. You know, I'm beginning to think it was a mistake to come out here. If I could get in my car, I'd say good riddance and leave this very minute."

Maxie deeply regretted never training Boo to kill on command. How could so much go so wrong in such a short period of time? Life had been so wonderfully uncomplicated when she'd walked into Howdy-Do Farm & Feed that morning. She'd just come from the bank and felt optimistic about her loan. Knowing both she and her cows would have money for food during the coming winter was a tremendous relief. She'd stopped at the donut shop and enjoyed the best apple fritter of her life. She was a contented woman.

And then Connor Garrett had stuck that lousy photograph under her nose and the bubble had burst.

"I don't like you," she told Connor succinctly, eyes narrowed. "You have no redeeming qualities."

"You don't know me yet," Connor pointed out. "It's much too soon to make a judgment call."

"Believe me, I know you as well as I'm going to."

He gave her a slow smile, a light of challenge in his dark eyes. "Wanna bet?"

While Maxie fortified herself with a Twinkie, Connor called a locksmith, but had to leave a message on his voice mail. When he hung up the phone, he looked at Maxie's stormy expression and shrugged helplessly. "What am I supposed to do? Is it my fault he's the only locksmith in Oakley? I'm sure he'll get back to me as soon as possible." Then, glancing beyond the kitchen window, he said, "I *suppose* I could wait outside. It looks like it might start raining again, but I certainly don't want to make you uncomfortable. Why don't I just wait on the porch swing? With any luck, the locksmith will get the message before I freeze to death. I'll just leave you in peace, all right? I don't want to be a bother...."

His wounded-puppy-dog act had no effect on Maxie. Still chewing, she shepherded Connor to the front door, pulling an afghan off the sofa along the way. "How considerate of you. Here, take this blanket. Wrap up snug and tight, and you probably won't freeze to death."

The glint of humor in Connor's expression faded abruptly. "The hell you say! You actually expect me to wait outside?"

"It was your idea, Mr. Garrett," Maxie said cheerfully. "I'll turn on the porch light so you won't be scared of the mutant rabbits. Bye-bye."

"Wait just a damn min—"

She shut the door on his protest without even the tiniest qualm of conscience. Then with an evil smile she turned on the porch light as promised. She knew how happy all the mosquitoes in a five-mile radius would be to have fresh meat on the porch.

She went back to the kitchen, choosing a juicy red apple from her fruit basket on the table. As she crunched on it, she found left-over roast chicken in the fridge and popped it into the microwave. She noticed the wind was turning rather fierce outside, rattling the kitchen windows in their frames.

What a shame, she thought. This would certainly ruin the last of her petunias in the garden.

She took her dinner back to the living room and flicked on the television. She always looked forward to Friday nights. There was a wonderful show on cable called *A Day in the Life of a Veterinarian*. It was very educational.

She had a pad of paper and pencil standing by in case she wanted to take notes. Tonight's episode dealt with "The Lurking Peril of Brucellosis."

And speaking of lurking perils…. For the first time since shoving Connor out the door, she glanced outside. There he was, huddled on the swing, the afghan pulled up to his eyeballs. He caught her eye and lifted the tips of his fingers far enough over the edge of the afghan to give a pathetic little wave. His new tangled dreadlocks gave evidence of the night wind's ferocity.

Maxie pulled a face as she heard the first drops of rain on her tin roof. Darn. Even she couldn't leave the man out in a rainstorm. She had a hard enough time leaving her cows outside during poor weather.

Scowling, she gestured for him to come inside. He hopped off the swing with the speed of a naughty little boy who'd been forced to sit in a corner, dashing across the porch and inside with the blanket held over his head. A freezing spray of rain and wind came inside with him.

"It's l-l-like a hurricane out there." His lips were frozen, the color faded to an interesting pale blue. "I hope you're happy."

"Of course I'm not happy," Maxie replied. "I

hate to see any animal suffer.'' Then, grudgingly, she gave up her place on the couch. ''Sit. I'll get you a cup of coffee.''

Connor burrowed into the sofa cushions, staring at the plate of chicken bones on the coffee table. ''You had chicken.''

''You're a regular Sherlock Holmes.''

''I love chicken.''

''I ate it all.''

''Of course you did,'' he muttered.

Maxie glared at him. ''What's *that* supposed to mean?''

''Nothing. Nothing at all. Don't worry about feeding me. I could stand to lose a few pounds.''

She took a deep breath. ''You do like playing the martyr, don't you? How on earth did a delicate soul like yourself ever survive playing professional football?''

He brightened considerably. ''You watched me play pro football?''

''Never. I just heard somewhere you played football before you became a reporter.''

''Well, I didn't play much,'' he admitted. ''Two games and I was out for the count. I blew out my knee when—''

''Do you want something to eat or not?'' Sitting there on the sofa with his wet mop of hair, melting brown eyes and touching tale of woe, he was almost endearing. Maxie couldn't afford to feel sympathetic. ''If you're really hungry, I'll fix you a plate of…something.''

He smiled weakly. ''Before you go…would you mind covering me with the blanket? I'm still a little chilled.''

"*Fine.*" She whipped the blanket out of his fingers, spreading it over him. "There we go, Mr. Garrett. All tucked in, nice and cozy. Is there anything else I can get for you? A hot-water bottle? Earmuffs? Perhaps a mustard poultice?"

"You wouldn't happen to have any brandy, would you?"

"Brandy? I can barely afford hay for my cows!"

"Don't get all prickly on me," he said. "You're probably tired. When you're well-rested, I'm sure you have a very nice personality."

"Nope," she retorted, heading for the kitchen. "This is as good as I get."

"And that's good enough," Connor murmured. He nearly snapped his neck following her exit. She had the most provocative sway to her hips, languid and sassy at the same time. He could just imagine her strutting the runway in a wispy dress that began late and ended early, her luscious hips rolling like thick honey, violet eyes half-closed, that swollen, edible mouth painted the sumptuous color of late-summer roses....

He grew conscious of a heated tightening in his groin. He tugged the blanket away from his body, sucking in a deep breath of air. For a man who'd just spent an hour in the deep freeze, he was suddenly and suffocatingly hot.

# Three

————

**W**hile Maxie was in the kitchen, Connor took the opportunity to nose about the room. Other than a single photograph on the mantel above the fireplace, there were no items of a personal nature, certainly no mementoes from Maxie's former life in the limelight. The lone photograph on the mantel was slightly yellowed; a picture of a young bride and groom posing in front of a tiny, white-spired country church. The groom looked highly uncomfortable. His mouth was pinched tight and the arm he had placed around his bride's waist looked as if it was made out of cardboard. The bride, however, was smiling lovingly at her husband, her dark curls loose and dancing in the sunlight. Her beauty was staggering. Like Maxie, she possessed incredible cheekbones, a generous mouth and stunning, wide-set eyes. Like mother, like daughter.

"What are you doing?" Maxie demanded.

Connor turned on his heel, flushing slightly. His reluctant hostess was standing in the doorway bearing a tray of food and a ferocious scowl.

"Nothing," he said, perhaps a shade too quickly.

"Nothing? You're snooping."

"Don't be silly." Connor avoided her accusing eyes, reclaiming his seat on the sofa. "Why did you put that picture on the mantel if you didn't want anyone to look at it?"

Maxie slammed the tray down on the coffee table. "I put it there so I could look at it. No one else, just me."

"That's your mother and father," Connor said, as if daring her to deny it. "Your mother was a beautiful woman."

"My mother still is a beautiful woman. Not that it's any concern of yours."

"Is this the way you treat all your visitors? It's not very hospitable, I'll tell you that."

"I've never had—" Too late, Maxie realized what she had been about to say. As did Connor, judging by the look of stunned incredulity on his face.

"No visitors?" he said. "*Ever?* That's a little tough to believe. Glitter Baby didn't exactly have a reputation as a loner. How long have you lived here?"

Maxie closed her eyes and counted to three. She was going to count to ten, but she lost her temper at three. "How long I've lived here is none of your damned business!" she snapped, stamping one booted foot on the floor. "*I'm* none of your business! My photographs are none of your business! Now eat your SpaghettiOs before I *pop* you one."

"Before you pop me one?" Connor's answering laughter died an abrupt death as he looked down at his dinner. "You weren't kidding," he said slowly. "You fixed me SpaghettiOs."

"Let me guess," Maxie said flatly. "You've never eaten SpaghettiOs."

"Well, of course I…no, actually I think you're right." Connor thought back to his mother's legendary Washington dinner parties. Never once did he recall seing SpaghettiOs on the menu. "This is a first for me. When I think of you out there in the kitchen, slaving over a hot pan of SpaghettiOs just for me…well, it does my heart good."

"You have quite an imagination, do you know that?" Maxie sat down on the arm of the sofa, her arms crossed over her chest. "I guess that's a prerequisite for your job."

"What's that supposed to mean?"

"You don't deal in facts. You deal in fabrication, anything to make a story more interesting."

Connor shrugged, making a production out of stirring his SpaghettiOs. "If you say so. You're quite defensive, do you know that? I think I understand why you never have visitors. Do you have any pepper to go with this?"

"Who on earth puts pepper on—" Maxie stood up, shaking her head. "Never mind. I'll be right back."

The instant Maxie left the room, Connor put his bowl of SpaghettiOs on the floor. Boo, who had been snoring beneath the coffee table, immediately sprang to life, gobbling down the major portion of Connor's dinner.

"What a good boy," Connor murmured. He took

the bowl back just as Maxie walked into the room. "I decided it didn't need pepper after all," he apologized. "Thank you, that really hit the spot. Now that I know what I've been missing all these years, I will certainly add SpaghettiOs to my—"

"Oh, save it," Maxie interrupted impatiently. "Boo has your dinner all over his face. I should have known you were a picky eater the moment I saw your jeans."

Dumbfounded, Connor stared at her. "My jeans? What about my jeans?"

"They're ironed," she retorted. "You're the first person I've ever met who irons a crease in their jeans."

"I do not iron my jeans," Connor said quite truthfully. His housekeeper did, albeit on his orders.

Maxie wrinkled her nose. "I'll bet you starch your undershorts and wear little suspenders to keep your socks up."

"Of course I don't starch my undershorts. What do you take me for?" There was nothing Connor could say about the "little suspenders." He owned several pairs for formal occasions. "Why am I the one being interrogated? I'm supposed to be asking you questions."

"Ask away," Maxie said. "Just don't expect me to answer."

They stared at one another while the silence lengthened. Her expression was defiant, his frustrated. Connor decided to go for his trump card.

"Two hundred fifty thousand dollars," he said. "A quarter of a million just for letting me tape one little interview. I don't know how much hay costs, but that's got to cover your expenses for quite a while.''

There had been a time in her life when a quarter of a million dollars was practically chump change. Maxie had no trouble remaining unimpressed. "No thanks," she said. "I can take care of my own money problems. I'd rather mortgage my land than sell my soul. Besides, why would you want to interview an obscure dairy farmer? You'd be a laughingstock."

This time Connor was the one counting to ten. "I know who you are," he said tightly. "You know I know who you are! Why keep playing this stupid game?"

"You're right," she said, twin spots of color burning high on her cheekbones. "It's a stupid game and I don't want to play any more. I'm going to get my jacket, then I'm driving you back to town. You can arrange to pick up your car tomorrow. Our discussion is over."

Maxie left the room in an indignant huff. Connor's thoughtful gaze followed her exit, then he stood up with a sigh and walked to the tiny coat closet and removed a metal hanger. He went outside and had the lock on his car open in less than two minutes. He walked back into the living room just as Maxie reappeared. She was wearing a denim jacket with sheepskin lining and had her cowboy hat planted firmly on her head once again.

"Where did you go?" she asked suspiciously.

"I thought I'd try opening the lock with a coat hanger," he explained, holding the bent hanger up like a trophy. "It worked, can you believe it? The rain has stopped, too. I guess my luck is turning."

"I'm happy for you," Maxie said acidly. "Why didn't you try to open the damn door before now?"

Connor grinned, his eyes lingering on her beautiful mouth. "Because I didn't want to open the damn door until now."

In the space of a few seconds, the atmosphere between them changed. What had been impersonal suddenly became quite personal. The air in the small living room seemed to change as well, becoming thicker and oxygen-sparse. Maxie was having trouble breathing. She stared at the boyish tangle of damp hair across his forehead and had the inexplicable urge to smooth it back. He looked like a mischievous child standing there with his dancing brown eyes and that stupid hanger in his hand. Her gaze dropped lower, to the snug jeans slung low on his narrow hips. A whisper of pure sensuality reared its dangerous head, sending a prickle of goose bumps over her skin.

"I want you to go now," she said hoarsely.

Connor nodded thoughtfully. "You're going to make this a struggle, aren't you?"

"I'm going to make it impossible. No interview, not now, not ever."

"I wasn't talking about the interview, pretty girl." He touched the tip of her nose with his finger. "You're enchanting, Maxie Calhoon. Prickly...but enchanting."

Maxie opened her mouth to say something, then closed it again. Her brain was stalled in neutral.

"I'm staying at the motel in Oakley for a couple of days," Connor said. "If you change your mind about the interview—"

"I won't."

"Here." He moved closer to her, then smiled as

she nearly jumped out of her boots. "I just wanted to give your hanger back," he explained, as if talking to a three-year-old. "I'll leave it on the sofa here, all right?"

"Fine. Go away."

Connor walked to the door, then paused. "You *are* Glitter Baby, aren't you?" he said without turning to look at her. "Just admit that much."

Strangely, Maxie's eyes filled with tears. No matter how far she ran, her alter ego still haunted her. She would never be judged for her own merits; she would always be Glitter Baby.

"I'm no one special," she said in a choked voice. "No one at all."

Connor hesitated, then walked outside, shutting the door quietly behind him.

Connor called Morris as soon as he returned to his motel room.

"I found her," he said without preamble.

His assistant's voice was groggy with sleep. "Do you have any idea what time...*what did you say?*"

"I found her."

"I hope this isn't a dream," Morris said fervently. "Texas doesn't agree with me. They grow mosquitoes here the size of cocker spaniels. I want to go back to Los Angeles. I miss the smog."

"Don't get too excited. She was less than enthusiastic about the interview."

"Less than enthusiastic? What does that mean?"

"It means she told me I was sneaky, opportunistic and underhanded. Oh, yeah...and oily."

"*Oily?* That's really low. What about the money you offered?"

"She turned it down. I was surprised, because she obviously needs some quick cash. She was talking about mortgaging her house to get through the winter."

"Damn. There's got to be something else we can do."

"I'll give it another shot tomorrow, but I'm not hopeful."

"What's she like?" Morris ventured. "Was it a letdown meeting her? There's no way she could be as gorgeous in person as she is in a photograph."

"She's actually quite amazing," Connor said quietly. "And no photograph could possibly do her justice."

Morris whimpered. "You dog. You have all the luck. I mean...you actually met her! *Glitter Baby.* What I wouldn't give to spend just one night with—"

"It's late and I'm beat," Connor said abruptly. For whatever reason, he didn't care to hear Morris fantasize about Maxie Calhoon. "I'll try my luck tomorrow and let you know what happens."

"Try your luck? You mean you're actually going to make a move on her?"

"Hell, Morris, get a grip. I meant I would talk to her about the interview. No wonder the woman disappeared. She was probably trying to get away from men like you. I'll call you tomorrow."

Connor hung up, then for reasons he couldn't fully explain to himself, pulled out his portfolio of Glitter Baby's photographs. He spread the pictures on his bed like an erotic quilt, studying them with intense new eyes. No man with a pulse could claim immunity to Glitter Baby's magnetic appeal. But suddenly

Connor was seeing someone else, a living, breathing soul with fears and human frailties, who was even more appealing. He knew what her husky velvet voice sounded like, and how it cracked when she got emotional. He knew how her hips moved when she walked and how her violet eyes darkened to blue fire when she lost her temper. Now she was something more than a heartbreakingly beautiful face and elegant body. She was a lady who could dress like a cowboy and look like an angel. She didn't seek admiration, attention or approval. She loved SpaghettiOs and animals and her independence. She drove a *truck,* for Pete's sake. As far as Connor knew, there wasn't another woman of his acquaintance who drove a truck. Jags, Corvettes, Mercedes…but not a single truck. The more he knew about Maxie, the more intriguing she became. What had made her turn her back on a hugely successful career? Even more fascinating was the quiet new life she had created for herself. Obviously finances were a concern, but she seemed unwilling to lean on her former fame to ease the burden.

Connor wondered if he would have had the courage to set off alone, leaving everything and everyone he had ever known. Even when he had been forced to quit football, his godfather had been right there for him, handing him a cushy job with a sweet paycheck. Truth be told, Connor had been spoiled rotten from day one, an only child who had always had whatever he wanted almost before he asked for it. He couldn't think of a time in his life when he'd waited for anything, much less worked for it. Football had been physically taxing, but he'd never considered it work. It had always been a game, and a game he was damn good at playing.

Connor shook his head, disturbed by the troubling stroll down memory lane. Where had all this damned introspection come from? Just because his life was easy didn't mean it lacked meaning. He'd done meaningful shows before. He'd interviewed a Nobel Prize winner once, a fellow who had managed to clone a goat. Surely that was worthwhile? Then there was the exposé on a certain television evangelist who had sticky fingers and a roving eye. That was public service by anyone's definition.

So why did he suddenly feel inadequate? What was it about Maxie Calhoon that prompted him to question his own values?

Again he let his gaze feast on the photographs on his bed. She was by far the most physically appealing woman on God's green earth. And yet…it had been the unexpected things that had touched him, the small surprises. The faint dusting of freckles on her sunburnt nose. The crooked little rows of vegetables in her rabbit-occupied garden. He'd set out to find the phenomenon known as Glitter Baby and instead met Maxie Calhoon, bless her feisty little soul.

Morris had been right. Connor *was* incredibly lucky.

The following morning, Maxie padded around her house in her pajamas, crouching like a commando and peering through each and every window. As far as she could see, she was alone. Still, she was nursing a bad case of the jitters. If one person could find her, other people could as well. Not to mention the fact that Connor Garrett could come back any time he pleased.

Sometime during the sleepless night, paranoia had moved in. Strangely enough, Maxie had never felt paranoid when she was modeling. Crowds, reporters, autograph seekers…they were all part of the charade. It was all make-believe.

Her life now was anything but a game. Every second was precious, every second mattered. She had responsibilities to take care of now, the most pressing of which were several cows who badly needed to be milked. Boo needed to be fed and the dishes from last night were still in the sink. At noon she was expected at the bank to sign the final papers on her mortgage. She told herself she couldn't afford to be distracted by what was probably a minor inconvenience, no matter how attractive that minor inconvenience had been.

Bolstered by her personal pep talk, she changed into her overalls and milked the cows, shared a hearty breakfast of scrambled eggs and cinnamon toast with Boo, then attacked the dirty dishes. She was feeling much more optimistic when the time for her appointment at the bank neared, and the sky still had not fallen in. Obviously she'd been overreacting. Life was good, and was going to get much better once she had expenses for the long Wyoming winter covered.

She exchanged her overalls for khaki pants and a black knit top, tugged a comb through her hair and left for the bank. It was a lovely day, the gold sunlight of autumn gilding the aspen and pine forests. Maxie slipped a Garth Brooks recording into the cassette deck and sang along at the top of her voice. Oh, if only her A-list former "friends" could see her now.

Oakley's bank was like every other establishment in town, small and personal. Maxie knew all three tellers, and smiled a friendly hello before poking her head into the bank manager's office.

"I'm here to sign my life away, Mr. Beasley," she said cheerfully. "Just hand me a pen and stand back."

Mr. Beasley wasn't smiling. He motioned for Maxie to sit in the chair opposite his desk. "There's been a problem," he said bluntly. "As I told you when you first filled out your papers, we run a last-minute credit check on anyone signing a mortgage loan. A lien has been placed on your property, Maxie. It's for quite a sizeable sum, almost ten thousand dollars."

Maxie blinked at him, stupefied. "What are you talking about? I have no debts whatsoever. I don't even possess a credit card."

Mr. Beasley consulted the notes on his desk. "The lien was placed by A & E Management. That's all the information I have."

Maxie felt a cold fist of dread closing around her stomach. When she'd first begun modeling, she'd been represented by A & E Management until she realized the agency was taking twice the sum agreed upon. Maxie had agreed not to sue them if they let her out of her contract. She hadn't heard a word from them since...until today. When Connor Garrett had found her, she'd expected others would follow. She'd been right, though she'd thought she'd have more time.

"I'm going to be sick," she moaned.

Mr. Beasley looked alarmed. "The restroom is just down the hallway."

"Mr. Beasley, everything I've worked for the past two years is riding on this loan."

"My hands are tied. I went so far as to call A & E to research the problem, but I was told any communication would have to be through their attorney. Perhaps if you hired an attorney, some sort of compromise—"

"I don't have the money for an attorney! If I did, I wouldn't need this loan."

"I'm sorry. I sympathize with you, but until you take care of the lien, there's nothing we can do. Perhaps you have a friend or relative who could help?"

"There's only my mother. She simply isn't in a position to lend me that amount of money." Maxie stood up, blinking away hot tears. "I'm not sure what I'm going to do, but I'll be in touch."

Outside, Maxie stood blinking on the steps of the bank and wondered where her beautiful day had gone. The sun was still shining brightly, but now it irritated her eyes and made her knit top heavy and itchy. The sweater was cashmere from a Calvin Klein collection and he would have vociferously denied the remotest possibility of skin irritation. Regardless, the damn thing suddenly itched. Inwardly Maxie consigned Calvin Klein, Connor Garrett and A & E Management to the devil. Oh yes, and Mr. Beasley, too.

She walked past her truck and wandered down Main Street, hands pushed in her pockets and head bent low. She walked right past her mother's antique store without stopping. She couldn't ask her mother for help. Natalie Calhoon barely made ends meet as it was. Without the refinancing, she was sunk. Her little dairy farm wouldn't come close to turning a profit for at least another year. The very idea of giving up her dream and selling off her cattle was anathema to her. She'd worked so terribly hard just to get where she was.

She paused by Corner Drug, known for a charming, old-fashioned soda fountain and homemade ice cream. Maxie was a devout believer in the healing power of empty calories, and suddenly craved a good strong sugar rush. She went inside, ordered the Pig's Dinner Banana Split and dug in with gusto. If she was going to be depressed, she would at least do it on a full stomach.

"So who's baby-sitting the moo cows?" a male voice drawled behind her. "Your canine garbage disposal?"

Maxie said a choice four-letter word beneath her breath, then swiveled on her stool to face Connor Garrett. "I don't want you to be a part of this day," she said. "It's already bad enough without you."

"We don't always get what we want, as I learned yesterday." He shrugged cheerfully, looking casually appealing in a white golf shirt that was a lavish contrast against his bronzed skin. His smile was a charming and elegant stretch, curling the edges of his honey-brown eyes. He wore black jeans this time, again perfectly creased. Today his sneakers were also black, and in mint condition. Naturally.

"Don't you ever get dirty?" Maxie asked him, finding his polish and poise extremely irritating. "Other than when you played football?"

Connor considered the question for a full ten seconds. "Once, when I was very young. I didn't like it."

"You're *strange*." Maxie did an about-face on the stool, giving the man her back. Instead of taking the not-so-subtle hint, he plopped down on the stool beside her and ordered a diet cola.

"Watching my figure," he told Maxie confidingly. He propped his elbows on the bar and rested his chin on his hands. "You remember how that is, don't you?"

She glared at him, her backbone stiffening. "Are you implying that I'm fat?"

"Certainly not."

Maxie poked him in the chest with a finger. "Because if you're implying that I'm fat, I really couldn't care—"

"I didn't call you fat." Connor regarded her with curious amusement. "How could someone be so astonishingly beautiful and so absolutely clueless at the same time? I didn't say you were fat. You have a good healthy appetite. What do you care, anyway? What I think doesn't matter, right?"

"Right. I don't care what anyone thinks." And to prove her point, Maxie ordered a root-beer float as a chaser. "Besides, sugar is recommended for depression."

"Who said that?"

"I did."

Connor nodded, as if she were making perfect sense. "And why are you depressed, if you don't mind my asking?"

"I do mind. Why would I confide in you? You're a perfect stranger."

"I wouldn't go so far as to say I'm perfect," he

replied modestly, "but you're entitled to your opinion." He gave her a dazzling smile. "Oh, I know why you're out of sorts today. You're sad because I'm going back to L.A. tomorrow."

"And now he's a comedian." Maxie sighed, not really in the mood for the verbal sparring. "Look, I'm not very good company right now. If you don't mind...?"

"Funny thing about that. You weren't the most cordial company last night either, and I can't think when I've been so entertained."

Maxie's expression was patently disbelieving. "Do you expect me to believe your life is boring?"

"Predictable, which is probably the same thing."

"Then do something *un*predictable now and then," she said. "Problem solved."

She was distracted by the arrival of her root-beer float. Connor watched as she dug into the creation with a plastic spoon, mesmerized by the way she smacked her lips. After a few moments, however, her love affair with her treat began to annoy him. He realized he had been dismissed in favor of her ice cream.

Irritated, he picked up a straw from the counter, tore off one end of the paper wrapper and lifted it to his lips. He blew, sending the empty wrapper sailing straight into Maxie's ear.

She yelped in surprise, turning her startled gaze in his direction.

Connor grinned from ear to ear, pleased with his little trick. "You said to do something unpredictable."

"Not to me," Maxie ground out. "Go do something unpredictable to someone else. I'm in the middle of a *crisis* here."

"You're in the middle of an ice-cream binge," Connor corrected. He reached out a finger, running it slowly along the edge of her lip. If possible, the brilliant color of her violet eyes intensified.

"You had a mustache," he said softly, holding her gaze while he licked the sweet foam off his finger. He became conscious of a new feeling stealing into his chest, a gentle emotion he was completely unfamiliar with. It took him a moment to put a name to it.

Tenderness. Its unexpected sweetness rippled through him, warming him inside and out. Connor's smile dropped by degrees from his lips. His eyes were lost in Maxie's, his heart beating a tattered, shallow rhythm.

Maxie lifted a hand that shook slightly and pointed to a root-beer stain on his shirt. "I've left my mark," she said, striving and failing to sound casual.

"I know." Connor's eyes looked slightly glazed. "I've known that for a while, but there doesn't seem to be anything I can do about it."

Maxie's lashes swept downward, shielding her expression. Connor had exhibited something unexpected today, something she very much feared was vulnerability. It made him very human and touchingly appealing.

It was a darn good thing he was going away tomorrow. His brash bravado she could have ignored forever, but this frank confusion went straight to her heart. She found a stiff smile and plastered it on her face. "Why did you come in here, anyway?"

"Why did I come in here?" It took him a moment

to remember. "Oh…razors. I need some disposable razors. Seeing you was an unexpected bonus. So, why don't you tell me about your terrible day?"

"It's personal."

"Personal or not, I'm a good listener."

Maxie shrugged. "I was supposed to sign papers for a mortgage loan today, but there's a fly in the ointment. I'll figure something out."

"I'm sorry things didn't go well." Connor forced himself not to press for an explanation. At least, not immediately. "Maybe it would help take your mind off your troubles if I took you out to dinner tonight. I can't offer SpaghettiOs, but the motel clerk told me the Trail's End Café is pretty good."

"Forgive me, but somehow I doubt having dinner with you will improve my situation. That's sort of like going from the frying pan to the incinerator." Her voice held the faintest hint of wistfulness. She hadn't had a date for two years, but it was best to be practical. Of course Connor had ulterior motives for asking her out, and it would be foolish of her to forget that.

"Even if I promised not to ask a single question?" he persisted, placing a sincere hand over his heart. Behind his back, he crossed his fingers. "Not a one?"

"You'd break that promise. Dissecting people is what you do for a living. Then you pin them up on your display board with all the parts identified, like a butterfly collection."

Indignant, Connor opened his mouth to argue, then shut it again with a snap. Damn it all, she was right. He *did* dissect people for a living. Put that way, it sounded less than admirable.

"I don't expect to host *Public Eye* forever," he blurted, wanting somehow to earn her approval. "I was thinking one of these days I might...try my hand at writing." He flushed, thinking how ridiculous he sounded. "I guess that's what everybody says. We all want to write the Great American Novel, right?"

"When did you decide this?" Maxie asked, intrigued despite herself.

"It's something I've been thinking about for a while. In the past few years I've discovered I like doing research. I thought I'd try a biography. Maybe. Someday."

"Maybe someday? You sound a little undecided."

"Actually I'm a lot undecided." He shrugged, stirring his soft drink with a straw. "It's just a thought."

"It's a good thought," Maxie said quietly. She smiled, her amazing eyes reflecting the soft light from a nearby window. "Just think, you'll be able to show the world you're more than just a pretty face."

"Oh, *now* I feel better," Connor muttered. "She thinks I'm pretty."

"Well, you are," Maxie went on blithely, enjoying his obvious discomfort. "You have the longest eyelashes I've ever seen. If I didn't know better, I'd swear you're wearing mascara."

"Quit it."

"And that golf shirt does absolutely wonderful things for your chest. You must work out a lot."

*"Quit it."*

"Don't you like compliments?"

"I like giving compliments. However, if you will have dinner with me tonight, you may compliment me up one side and down the other. I'll even wear something form-fitting.''

"Tempting as that sounds, I can't.'' Maxie's smile faded as she slipped off the stool and put a five-dollar bill on the counter. There was an undercurrent of friendliness going on here, and she couldn't afford to be friends with Connor Garrett. "It's too complicated, Connor. We both know the real reason you're here. Taking me to dinner isn't going to make me change my mind about the interview."

Connor's half smile fell short of reaching his eyes. "That's that, then?"

"You've been a worthy adversary," Maxie added ruefully. "I wish you the best with—"

"Wait." He touched her arm briefly. "I'll be here until tomorrow. If for any reason you change your mind about the interview or the dinner, please call me."

"Goodbye, Connor."

*"Wait."* He had a terrible feeling if he let her walk out the door, he'd never see her again. He frantically scanned his brain for a good reason to delay her, even for a few seconds. "I have one last question for you."

She raised a droll glance heavenward. "I should have known."

"Uhhmm…if you *were* the young woman known once upon a time as Glitter Baby, your christened name was Frances Calhoon. How did you come up with the name Maxie?"

"I suppose I *might* have gone with my middle name, which just *might* have been the name my parents called me, anyway." Her serene smile reminded Connor of the Mona Lisa. "But that's just a guess."

Connor watched her walk out of the drugstore with his mouth hanging open. Her middle name? It was that simple? Her middle name?

"Sir? Anything else you want?" This from the teenage waitress, who sounded quite put out. Connor blinked at her, wondering how long she had been standing there.

Connor couldn't think of a single reason in the world to smile, but he managed one anyway. "No," he said quietly. "Nothing I can have, at any rate."

He called Morris the moment he returned to his hotel room. "Why didn't we know her middle name was Maxie?"

"I'm not sure," Morris said carefully. "Is this a trick question? Does my paycheck depend on my answer?"

"Her middle name is Maxie. And get this—she's listed in the damned Oakley phone book, plain as day. Maxie Calhoon."

Silence. Then, hesitantly, "We probably should have known that. How did you find out?"

"She told me," Connor said flatly. "Which seems to be the only way I can get any dependable information on her."

Morris cleared his throat. "Not very sporting of her, to use her own name. Obviously, she doesn't play fair. Then again," he added philosophically, "neither do we."

"What do you mean by that?"

"Oh…nothing, really. Just the nature of the business, you know. The sly bird gets the worm."

"Whatever," Connor muttered, rubbing the back

of his neck tiredly. "I gave her until tomorrow to change her mind, but it's not going to happen."

"Never say never. Miracles still happen. Besides, I've talked to Alan Greenspan's people. I think we could work something out."

"Go after Glitter Baby, come back with Alan Greenspan. It will take me some time to adjust to that one, Morris."

"Is it that big a deal?" Morris queried hesitantly. "I mean…we tried, but we can't win them all. If it doesn't work out, just forget about her and move on."

Sam glanced at the bedside table where Maxie's photographs were scattered. Every picture was seared into his soul, every expression memorized. And yet…they didn't do her justice, they didn't begin to capture the essence of the woman. She was inside him like a powerful drug, heating his blood, waking him up to the unsatisfied shell of his own need.

"I can't," he said softly. "I can't."

# Four

**R**ather than returning to her truck, Maxie walked to the end of Main Street where her mother's antique shop was located, tucked cozily between the Anglers' Inn and the Oakley post office. She pushed the screen door open with the heel of her hand, then nearly jumped out of her skin when the shrill sound of a rooster crowing assaulted her ears. "Yikes! What the devil?"

"Maxie, is that you? Honey, I'm sorry." Natalie came dashing in from the back room, a blue gingham scarf wildly askew on her flying dark hair. She had a smear of dirt on her chin, which was typical, and her hands were painted green, which was not. "Ralph Henley hooked up this gosh-awful contraption to the door this morning. He calls it a Ring-a-Ding-Doodle and says every shopkeeper must have one for security. I couldn't refuse it, but I *am* planning on accidentally breaking it later today. How are you, sweetie?''

''You and your boyfriends,'' Maxie teased, giving her mother a hug. Natalie was not only one of the few available women in town, but also happened to resemble Sophia Loren in her younger days. The poor widowers and bachelor farmers of Oakley had been throwing themselves at her right and left for nearly three years now. Oddly enough, Natalie was still bewildered by the attention.

''Ralph is not a boyfriend,'' Natalie replied, ''as you very well know. He's just a very nice fellow who invents really bad things. Honey, scratch my nose. It itches, and I'm covered with paint. Do you like the shade of my hands? It's a nice color, don't you think?''

''Very attractive.'' Maxie did as she was told, shaking her head at her mother's bright-eyed enthusiasm. In her worn jeans and sweatshirt, Natalie looked more like Maxie's sister than her mother. ''What are you working on today?''

''Oh, I've had the *best* morning. I found a lovely old cedar chest at the swap meet. I'm painting it sage green and it's turning out beautifully. It's on the sunporch; come and take a look.''

''Actually,'' Maxie sighed with resignation, hating to put a damper on her mother's high spirits, ''we need to talk. I had a little bit of a surprise yesterday, and I thought you might be able to give me some advice.''

Natalie's observant blue gaze studied her daughter's expression. ''This isn't a happy surprise, is it? Hang on, I'll go wash my hands and then we'll have a good chat.''

Maxie looked about the shop while her mother was out of the room. It was a marvelous, magical place, crowded with everything from old-fashioned bird-baths to Victorian stained-glass lamps. For twenty-four years Natalie had been a quiet, hard-working farmer's wife, with neither the time nor the opportunity to follow her own dreams. Since becoming a widow, however, she'd taken on the world with open arms and a hopeful heart. Like Maxie, Natalie Calhoon had turned out to be a survivor.

"Here, I brought you a cola." Natalie carried one can for herself and one for her daughter, with a bag of pretzels under her arm. "Now come and sit down and tell me absolutely everything."

Thirty minutes later they were both on their second soft drink, the pretzels were gone and Maxie's mother knew absolutely everything. Natalie was quiet, gazing into space while she mulled over all that her daughter had said. "Do you want my honest opinion?" she said finally, meeting her daughter's troubled gaze.

"Of course I do."

"I'd look on this interview with Connor Garrett as a godsend. With the amount of money he's offering, you won't have to refinance your farm and you can pay off the lien on the property as well. It's as easy as that."

Maxie blinked at her mother. "What? After everything I've gone through to start a new life, you think I should resurrect Glitter Baby?"

"Glitter Baby can't hurt you anymore," Natalie said calmly. "There was a time when you needed anonymity, a time when you needed to heal. You've done that, sweetheart. You're stronger now. You

have confidence in yourself, and you love this new
life you've built. Connor Garrett can't take that away
from you, Maxie. No one can."

"That's hard to believe," Maxie murmured, thinking back to the fragile, battle-scarred woman who
had quite literally run for her life two years earlier.
It simply hadn't occurred to her that she might have
finally gained the strength and understanding to rec-
oncile her past and her future. "You really think I
should do the interview?"

"Why ever not?" Natalie asked simply. "Show
the world what I already know—Maxie Calhoon not
only survived, but she did it beautifully."

"But afterwards…you know as well as I do the
reporters and photographers will be coming out of
the woodwork."

Natalie shrugged. "Probably, but the curiosity will
be short-lived. Darling, I hate to tell you this, but
raising milk cows is not the stuff miniseries are made
of. You have become," Natalie lowered her voice
theatrically, *"ordinary."*

Maxie's lips quirked into a faint smile that grew
into a full fledged grin as laughter overtook her.
"Good heavens, you're right! I'm ordinary. Isn't that
the most wonderful thing?"

Laughing, Natalie threw her arms around her
daughter and hugged her tightly. "Poor Connor Garrett. He doesn't have a clue what he's up against."


So this was the wild, wild west.

As Connor hesitated in the doorway of the Silver
Horseshoe Bar, he realized two things. One, Maxie
Calhoon had not arrived yet. She was the sort of
person who stood out from the crowd, regardless of

how hard she tried to blend in. And two, he seemed
to be the only male in the place who wasn't wearing
a cowboy hat.

He briefly regretted the impulse that had prompted
him to don a peach-colored knit shirt. Such a shirt
was perfectly acceptable in a California sushi bar, but
the Silver Horseshoe subscribed to another dress
code entirely. Everybody looked like Clint East-
wood, with sun-browned skin, pearl-buttoned shirts
and tight-fitting Wranglers. Everyone but Connor,
who felt like a pink flamingo in a sea of faded denim.

He took a seat at the far end of the bar and ordered
a whiskey rather than his usual martini. He never
drank whiskey, but in all the western movies he had
ever watched, everyone who patronized a saloon
drank whiskey. As far as Connor could recall, John
Wayne had never sidled up to the bar and ordered a
martini. He sipped the drink slowly, pulling a face
each time he raised the glass to his lips. Still, he
forced himself to continue drinking until a pleasant
warm rush was pumping through his veins and the
tension in his shoulders eased up a bit. He'd been on
edge ever since Maxie's phone call earlier that afternoon. She had asked him to meet her for drinks at
the Silver Horseshoe. When he'd questioned whether
it was business or pleasure, she'd merely replied,
"I'm not out to seduce you, if that's what you
mean."

Connor had no idea where his ordinarily unflap-
pable composure had run off to. He felt out of his
element, not at all knowing what to expect. He could
handle politicians, actors, writers and rock stars, but
one former supermodel known as Glitter Baby

seemed to have him on a very short leash. Every time he turned around, she was throwing him a curve.

And speaking of curves...Connor's head swiveled as he heard the front door swing open. Maxie stood in the fuzzy red light from a neon sign on the wall, looking around the room. She wasn't dressed as a farmer tonight. No hat, no grimy boots, no ponytail. She wore her hair loose and wild around her shoulders, huge silver hoop earrings glinting through the strands. Fitted black jeans were paired with a long-sleeved turquoise tank top, lovingly outlining every curve from her ankles to her breasts. A silver chain belt inlaid with turquoise stones glittered at her waist.

Connor felt his throat go desert-dry and his heartbeat kick into a frantic tango. He tossed back the last of his whiskey and thought, *I'm in deep trouble here.*

She waved as she caught sight of him at the bar, crossing the room through an obstacle course of tables and chairs. Her walk was a study of beauty in motion, her long legs moving with innate grace, shoulders instinctively back and her head high. Connor watched every weathered cowboy in the room stare at this exotic creature in their midst. He took a primitive satisfaction in knowing she was walking towards *him.*

"You don't even notice it, do you?" he said by way of greeting, rather proud his voice didn't quiver.

Maxie slipped on the stool next to him, folding her arms on the bar. "Don't notice what?"

"The sudden surge of testosterone in the room. Every eye in the place is on you and you don't even blink."

"Battle scars from doing too many fashion shows. When you're on a runway in front of hundreds of people, you learn to block everything out except getting from point A to point B without tripping and falling flat on your face.''

"So she finally admits it," Connor murmured softly, his eyes widening with surprise. He held out his hand. "Nice to meet you, ma'am. I'm Connor Garrett. And you are…?"

She hesitated a moment, then took a deep breath and shook his hand. "Frances Maxine Calhoon," she responded. "But you can call me Maxie."

He felt a wave of soft delight go through him, knowing she was finally letting down her barriers. "And what line of work are you in, Maxie?"

She got a gaint, rueful grin. "Cows."

His smile matched hers. "Really? What do you do with them?"

"Milk 'em."

"How creative. Do you enjoy your work?"

"Very much," she said quietly, looking down at their clasped hands. "Connor?"

"What?"

"Could I have it back?"

"What?"

"My hand."

He cleared his throat, and released his grip. "Sorry. It's not every day I meet a genuine cow milker. I'm somewhat in awe." This, at least, was the absolute truth. He was completely lost in the curious demanding feelings that filled the air between them. Lost in the impossibly lush curves of her pink-tinted lips. Lost in the thick-lashed violet eyes he could never get away from in his mind.

The bartender planted himself in front of Maxie,

staring for a full thirty seconds before he found his voice. "What can I get you?"

"A piña colada," she said. Then, when the bartender remained frozen in place, "Is there a problem with that?"

"There's no problem yet," Connor interjected in a smooth voice that barely disguised his irritation. "But there will be if he doesn't pull himself together in the next two seconds. *Piña colada,* buddy."

The bartender blinked and bustled away. Maxie turned a startled gaze on Connor. "What got into you? That wasn't very polite."

Connor shrugged. "Considering what I wanted to do to him," he replied, "it was extremely polite. His mother should have taught him better manners."

Quite simply, Maxie did not know what to make of him. It seemed Connor's confident, composed exterior disguised a man who was very human. "You aren't at all what you appear to be," she said thoughtfully.

"Who is?" Connor replied. "We all wear different masks for different occasions. It's the way of the world."

"Your world, maybe," Maxie replied, staring down at her hands on the bar. "Not mine. Not anymore. Living like that takes too great a toll. There's no joy in life when you're living a lie."

He could tell this level of honesty was hard for her, yet she seemed determined to drop any further pretense. "Why did you call me, Maxie? Why the sudden about-face?"

She took her time before answering. "Let's just say I find myself between a rock and a hard place.

As things stand, I don't have any choice but to go ahead with the interview."

Connor stared at her. "You continually take me by surprise," he said finally, shaking his head. "This afternoon you say goodbye and good riddance forever, tonight you agree to do the interview. Not that I'm not delighted, but...what's going on?"

"I changed my mind."

"Are you sure that's what you want?"

She shrugged. "I'm sure it's what I *don't* want, but I have no choice. As long as you agree to a few ground rules, we'll go ahead and get it over with."

Connor's ego gave a little wince. "You know, maybe you'll find it won't be such a terrible experience. Hell, you might even enjoy it. People have said I make it easy for them to talk, painless even."

"That's not necessarily a good thing. If you're not careful, words can be twisted and used against you. It happened to me over and over. People love tawdry scandals far more than simple truths."

"I wouldn't do that to you," he said quietly.

She smiled at the bartender as he delivered her drink. He was very careful not to smile back, keeping a wary eye on Connor. "I suppose that remains to be seen," she replied matter-of-factly, pulling the paper umbrella from her drink and twirling it between two fingers. "I won't put on any pretenses. I'm no longer in the business of people-pleasing. I still have a farm to take care of, cows to milk, a garden to weed, all that sort of scintillating stuff. You'll have to work around me."

"No problem. Anything else?"

She met his eyes squarely. "You won't reveal my exact whereabouts. You can say I'm somewhere in the west, but don't be more specific than that. I don't have an agent anymore, I don't have bodyguards, alarm systems, a doorman or a concierge. This is a whole new ballgame. It's just me against the world now, and I have to be careful.''

He thought back a couple of years, to the times when her photograph was just about everywhere he looked. The gossip rags had been full of nightmare stories about stalkers, obsessed fans and jealous boyfriends. Connor was familiar with notoriety, being a semi-famous person himself, but Maxie's career had garnered her far more than professional fame. The public had become obsessed with the beautiful young wild child. Every movement she had made was news, every magazine cover featuring her face was an automatic bestseller. He thought he understood her determination to remain lost. ''I'll sign a contract stating just that, as will my assistants and every person in my camera crew. I'll make this as easy on you as possible, Maxie.''

''Oh, and one more thing.'' She smiled easily at him, a cool veteran of thousands of such negotiations. ''I want three hundred fifty thousand.''

Connor flinched, knowing the money would come out of his own pocket if necessary. ''Ouch. You're very young to drive such a hard bargain. Anything else?''

She shrugged, turning her attention to her drink. ''No. Believe it or not, I'm not greedy. I need money to pay expenses until the farm starts making a profit. I also need a bull for my love-starved cows. Excellent bloodlines don't come cheap.''

Connor stared at her, wondering how on earth to respond to that. ''You're a unique person,'' he commented finally, aware this was a vast understatement. "Before you launch into the finer points of breeding cows, would you like to dance?"

The question seemed to startle her. She'd been perfectly in control until that point, keeping things on a cool, professional footing. He'd just kicked her legs out from under her.

"Please?" Connor cajoled, smile lines curling his soft dark eyes. "We really ought to become better acquainted before filming starts. Everything will go much more smoothly if we're comfortable with each other."

"I'm comfortable right now," Maxie muttered. This was a bald-faced lie. Since walking into the bar, she'd been only too aware of Connor's powerful physical presence. His sun-streaked, golden-brown hair was long enough in back to brush the collar of his shirt, lending him a boyish sort of charm. His features were full of bright expression, his eyes probing deeply each time he looked at her. His shirt draped loosely over well-sculpted muscles, soft blue jeans belted low and tight on a narrow waist. A perfect male animal. What stud fees he could command, she thought wistfully, then choked on her drink as sudden laughter doubled her over.

"What?" Connor asked, clearly confused.

"I spend too much time with my cows," she managed, still laughing. "I've become a little strange."

"More than a little." He stood up, tapping her on the shoulder. "On your feet, strange one. You're either going to dance with me or with Wyatt Earp over there. He's heading this way."

Maxie looked over her shoulder, grimacing as she spotted a tall, dark and not-at-all handsome cowboy bearing down on her. "I forgot what bars are like," she grumbled, slipping off her bar stool. "The music just changed. I hope you know how to line dance, city boy."

Connor eyed the long row of dancers with some apprehension. "It looks like something out of *Riverdance*. You think we can bluff our way through it?"

"Are you kidding? I haven't been in a bar for two years. And when I did dance…well, it wasn't like that."

"Show me."

Clasping her hand lightly, he led her onto the floor. They found a quiet corner free from stomping cowboy boots, where they could move as they liked.

And then Maxie started to move.

Connor danced as he always had, rather conservatively, but with lazy confidence. Maxie, however, moved with innate, primitive rhythm, hips swaying seductively and eyes half-closed as she concentrated on the music. She seemed to lose herself instantly in the dance, a luscious little smile on her lips as her back arched effortlessly to the beat. She tipped her head backward until her hair nearly reached her waist, then tossed her hair forward with a spirited, feline grace. She was totally absorbed in her romance with the rhythm.

Connor's eyes filled with smoldering heat, his mouth slightly parted as he watched her. Her dance was having quite an effect on him—his jeans were fitting a bit more snugly than they had thirty seconds earlier. She wasn't dancing for an audience; she was dancing for herself, absorbed in her own private ritual. He could imagine her dancing like this a hundred times in the past, a sought-after celebrity seizing the chance to lose herself, if only for a few minutes. He was jealous of every single man who had ever watched her move with so much simmering emotion.

"Heaven help me," he said.

"What?" She opened her eyes fully, shaking her head to show she couldn't hear him. "Music's too loud," she pantomimed.

He grinned, enjoying the momentary freedom to say exactly what he wanted to say. "Maxie, I want you."

She shrugged, holding up her hands. "Can't hear you. Tell me later."

Connor nodded, the corners of his mouth lifted in an evocative, knowing curve. *I will, sweetheart. I will.*

It was long past midnight when Connor walked Maxie to her truck. The night air hit their heated skin with a bracing coldness, stealing their breath. Try as he might—and he didn't try very hard—Connor couldn't help but notice Maxie's nipples growing hard beneath her clingy tank top.

"You should have brought a coat," he said, quite happy that she hadn't.

"I didn't expect to be here this late." She paused by her truck, her face illuminated in the light from a streetlamp. "I think this is the first time in two years I've stayed up past the ten o'clock news. I'm going to hate myself come milking time."

"If you're trying to convince me you didn't enjoy yourself tonight, forget it."

"It's been a long, long time since I relaxed like

that. I have to admit, I enjoyed dressing like a girl again.''

''Are you thinking about trading in your overalls for dresses and heels?''

''Absolutely not. My cows would never recognize me.'' She gave him a wonderful smile, unguarded and engaging. ''I figured something out in the last couple of years. Too much of anything breeds boredom. Good times have to be balanced with the ordinary to get the full effect.''

Maxie's easy smile was full of her own special brand of magic, her eyes luminous. Connor ached to touch her. Under the circumstances, however, he contented himself with nipping the tip of her nose with his fingers. ''You have a great deal of wisdom for someone your tender age.''

She laughed, shaking her head. ''My tender age? I'm twenty-four going on forty-four. Believe me, I haven't a scrap of wide-eyed illusion left.'' They reached her truck and she turned to face him, leaning her back against the driver's door. ''I'm not complaining. When you realize the big things in life are usually a disappointment, you finally learn to appreciate the little things.''

Connor wanted her to go on talking—and smiling—forever. Happiness, like every other emotion, looked good on her. ''Like what?''

''Sunsets,'' she said promptly. ''The taste of fresh lemonade. The smell of the sky after rain. *Brownies.*'' She paused, planting her hands on her hips. ''What have I said to set you off laughing like that?''

''Nothing. Everything…the way you say things.'' Connor could hardly get the words out. He cupped her shoulders with his hands, still laughing. ''You make it all new again, Maxie. I thought I'd seen everything, but I'd never seen you, had I?''

Maxie had to smile as well, taking in the picture he made with his knit shirt pulled out over his jeans and his hair every which way from dancing. His all-American good looks were gilded with lamplight, soft and sensual. He'd never looked as appealing to her as he did in that unguarded moment.

Connor lost his laughter suddenly, his eyes taking on a sleepy intensity. Maxie sensed the change in him and tried to move out of his grasp, but he stopped her with a soft, ''Don't. Please don't.''

She had no idea why she did as she was told. Too many drinks perhaps, she thought numbly. Her lips parted as his face filled her vision, her gaze settling on his mouth. A car nearby pulled out of the parking lot, its headlights briefly illuminating them with blinding honesty. Maxie saw the naked need in his eyes and felt an answering response flaring deep within. His hands moved upwards to frame her face, his touch as light as the breeze that swirled around them. He took less than a step, bringing his hips gently into contact against hers. The answering vibration in the pit of Maxie's stomach made her gasp.

''Don't be afraid,'' he whispered, running his thumb lightly along the curve of her lower lip. Maxie nervously touched her tongue to her dry lips, tasted his skin and shivered. Her eyes were enormous.

''This isn't...'' She tried to assemble her scrambled wits, tried to remember whatever it was she had been about to say.

''What?'' he asked, bringing his mouth a fraction of an inch from hers. ''This isn't...?''

''This isn't...you shouldn't—''

He stopped her words with the butterfly touch of his lips settling on hers. It was a gentle, whisper-soft kiss, lighter than the moonlight. His tongue traced the edges of her mouth ever so gently, memorizing the sinfully sweet shape. It took all his willpower not to deepen the contact, every ounce of determination he possessed to pull back from her warm body and moist, parted lips.

"Thank you," he managed unevenly.

Maxie sagged against the truck, her legs feeling like they were made of butter. Warm butter. "For what?"

"Calling me. Dancing like a sorceress. Breathing. Take your pick." He moved her to one side, opening the truck door. "Time to go, Maxie. Right now, while I'm still behaving myself."

Maxie did as she was told, moving like a sleep-walker.

"Seat belt," he said, while he was still holding the door open.

She did up her seat belt with clumsy fingers.

"You're unusually cooperative tonight. What if I asked you…?"

Seized by some wild, dangerous impulse, Maxie lifted her chin and stared him straight in the eyes. "Asked me what, Connor?"

"Go home, little girl." His voice was suddenly tight and soft, a muscle working in his cheek. "We'll talk tomorrow."

For a moment she could only stare at him, feeling strangely exhilarated. It had been so long since she'd been conscious of her power as a woman, but she felt it tonight. Oh boy, did she.

Connor's eyes narrowed. "Now," he said.

Something in his expression told her he meant business. Maxie pulled the keys from their hiding place in the sun visor and started the truck. Connor shut her door with an excess of force, being careful not to look at her again. Then, because he knew his own limits, he turned and walked away without a backward glance.

# Five

During milking the following morning, Maxie used the cows as an audience and nervously rehearsed a few possible greetings for Connor when he arrived.

"How pleasant to see you again." No, too formal.

"Hello there, Connor. Isn't it a lovely morning?" Ugh. Too perky.

"Are you as tired as I am?" Yech, too honest. She didn't want the man knowing she'd tossed and turned all night.

Eventually she decided to play it by ear. She told herself she wasn't as much anxious as she was uncertain. Connor had managed to shake her and tempt her and please her all at once, the emotions stubbornly lingering right through the night and on into the sunrise. Her skin still prickled with chills when she recalled the brief sensation of his lips on hers.

She felt as if a secret place inside her was somehow waking after being asleep a long time.

Noon came and went and still there was no sign of Connor. Maxie's uncertainty gradually evolved into irritation. Why was she allowing Connor Garrett to influence her routine? She'd been perfectly happy with her life before she met him, and if she expected to be perfectly happy after he left, she'd better get a grip on herself.

With a fresh sting of blood heating her cheeks, she stomped outside and started weeding the garden with ferocious energy. Dirt was flying every which way; poor Harvey's thick bunny fur was soon clotted with soil from ears to tail. Boo sensed his human's unsettled mood, and quickly disappeared behind the shed for a peaceful, dirt free afternoon nap. Boo was a lover, Maxie thought ruefully, not a fighter.

She'd done a fair bit of damage to the weeds when she heard the sound of a car coming up the lane. She looked up, her stomach doing an odd little flip when she caught the flash of a familiar canary yellow rental car through a line of aspens. She had an urge to smooth her hair and defiantly resisted it. She reminded herself she was no longer haunted by that hobgoblin of the supermodel's mind—appearance.

She watched the car turn down her drive, then went back to work with a renewed zeal and a quickened heartbeat. Weeds flew, half-grown carrots scattered, even a tiny stake bearing an identifying vegetable seed packet went up and over her shoulder. This flurry of activity was more than even the usually placid Harvey could take. Nose twitching nervously, he scuttled for cover beneath a friendly head of cabbage.

A car door slammed and slow footsteps crunched on the gravel. Maxie forced herself to count to ten before turning around. Connor was backlit by a halo of afternoon sun, a faceless shadow figure with broad shoulders and narrow hips.

"You," he said with amusement, "have dirt on your nose."

Maxie shaded her eyes with her gloved hands, blinking him slowly into focus. "Why, it's you," she remarked with feigned surprise. "I'd forgotten you were dropping by."

Connor's smile clearly gave the impression she wasn't fooling him for a minute. "I suppose I should have called first," he said with exaggerated regret. "My deplorable manners. Shall I go back to town and give you a ring?"

"Very funny. It would serve you right if I told you to go ahead and..." Her voice trailed off into dazed silence. Connor still had the same voice, the same longish mane of hair, the same butter-won't-melt-in-my-mouth expression on his face. From the neck down, however, he was someone else. "Good heavens," she finally managed. "You've turned into John Wayne."

"I decided I needed a new look," Connor announced, rocking happily back and forth on his feet. "How do you like it?"

Maxie stood up, automatically brushing the soil from her overalls as she gawked at him. She was truly speechless. All traces of the California-cool television personality had been erased. He wore a plain white T-shirt with a John Deere logo on the chest. Over this he wore an open denim jacket, the fabric obviously prewashed to a nicely faded summer blue. His skin tight jeans matched the jacket perfectly. Brand new cowboy boots completed the ensemble, the shiny alligator skin dulled a bit by a thin layer of dust from the gravel walkway. He looked like he was all geared up for a Fourth of July rodeo. The only jarring note was his mirrored aviator sunglasses.

"You're not Connor Garrett," she said. "Who are you and what have you done with him?"

He grinned, obviously enjoying his opportunity to play cowboy. "Look here," he pointed out, indicating his creaseless jeans. "I'm practically *wrinkled*. It's too warm today to wear the jacket, but I wanted you to get the full effect." He shrugged out of the jacket, hooking it on his thumb and tossing it over his shoulder. "I feel like getting on a horse and herding something."

"I don't have horses," Maxie mumbled. Her attention was riveted by Connor's new clothes—or, rather, by the way his new clothes fit his sculpted body. The T-shirt was smaller than his usual loose-fitting golf shirts, showing every rounded curve of his beautifully defined chest muscles. His jeans left nothing to the imagination. He was in incredible shape, truly *incredible* shape. What was it about lean hips and powerful thighs that sent a woman's imagination into overdrive? She was a lustful wench, Maxie thought despairingly. Not that she'd ever admit it to Cowboy Connor.

"So what do you think?" he prodded, pulling the sunglasses down on his nose and peering at her over the top. "I kind of stood out like a sore thumb at the bar last night. This is better, right? Do I blend?"

Maxie smiled weakly. "Just like one of the local

boys. All you need now is a handlebar mustache and a bouncing beer belly and you'll fit right in.''

Grinning widely, he pushed the sunglasses back in place. "What with the interview and everything, I don't know if I'll have time to develop the beer belly, but I'll give it my best shot."

Interview. That single word took the warmth out of Maxie's eyes. She'd forgotten for a moment that Connor was here on business. The object of his interest was not Maxie Calhoon. If she wanted to keep her heart in one piece, she would do well to remember that. "Oh yes, the exclusive Glitter Baby exposé. How could I have forgotten? When do you want to get started?"

Connor looked at her quizzically. One moment she was warm and natural, the next she might have been a million miles away. "You know, we were actually doing pretty well there for a few seconds. What did I say to turn you into the ice queen again?"

She merely shrugged, a gesture that sent one strap of her overalls sliding off her shoulder. She pushed it back again automatically, stubbornly maintaining her silence. She had no clue how endearing the childish gesture was to Connor, how adorable she looked to him with her soiled overalls, smudged nose and flowered gardening gloves that were obviously much too big for her small hands.

"One baby step forward, two giant steps backward," he sighed. "Maxie, I had an idea this morning. Actually, more of a revelation."

"A revelation?" Her beautiful eyes chided him. "I doubt that."

"You doubt everything, kiddo. We're going to have to work on that. Anyway, here's what I propose: my camera crew won't be here for a couple of days. I think we should use the time to get to know each other, to establish some kind of trust. The interview will be much easier for you if you're at ease.''

Maxie dipped her head, drawing circles in the dirt with the toe of her sneaker. ''Don't worry about me. I've given hundreds of interviews. I figure I can handle one more.''

Connor took a deep, let's-try-this-again breath. ''How about friendship, then? Or does Maxie Calhoon have all the friends she needs?''

Maxie pondered this, head still bent. Then, her voice not much louder than a whisper, said, ''Are you sure that's who you want to get to know? Maxie Calhoon?''

''Maxie Calhoon, milker of cows, tender of rabbits and lover of SpaghettiOs. That's the woman I'd like to get to know.''

She pulled off her gloves, slapping them against her thigh to shake off the dirt. Still she avoided his eyes. ''You're likely to be disappointed. She's nothing out of the ordinary.''

''She's anything but ordinary,'' he replied. He dropped his jacket in the dust and took hold of her shoulders. He could feel the tension jump in her body, as if an electric current was silently shivering through her muscles. His thumbs began to massage her shoulders in small circles. ''I just realized something. We always talk about Maxie as if she was a third person. It's almost as if you don't know her very well yourself yet.''

''You're probably right,'' Maxie said, unable to control the tremor in her voice. She wondered if Connor had any idea what his touch did to her. "Up until a couple of years ago, she was a complete stranger to me."

Connor didn't miss the nerve chills in her voice, and he was encouraged. It meant, he hoped, that on some level, she was responding to him. He only had two days, three at the most, before they were inundated with his people. It was amazing what a small army an hour long special commanded. And there was so much he wanted, *needed,* to learn about her before then.

He bent his head close to hers, his breath stirring the tendrils of hair over her ears. "I have a picnic in the car," he whispered, as if confiding a great secret. "Not just your ordinary picnic, either...it's a *chocolate* picnic."

"I've never had one of those before," Maxie gasped. She was becoming weak all over from the achingly pleasurable sensation of his breath stirring in her ear. Tattered heartbeats skipped in her chest, leaving her sparse of oxygen. She looked over Connor's shoulder, watching the breeze dance with the long meadow grass in the pasture. Nothing much had changed in her life the past couple of days. The farm was the same, the cows still required milking, the autumn leaves still blazed gold and red on the aspen trees. Nothing had changed...and everything had changed.

"I'm taking you away from your ranch, your garden and your cows," Connor told her, rubbing his nose ever so lightly against the baby-soft skin of her neck. "Too much work makes Jill a dull girl. Besides, you haven't lived until you've had a chocolate picnic."

She pulled back just far enough to look in his eyes. "Have you?"

He cocked his head curiously. "Lived?"

She smiled faintly. "Had a chocolate picnic."

"No." He kissed her forehead lightly, then forced himself to step back from her. Even without makeup, her incredible eyes never lost their spellbinding appeal. Her thick, spiky lashes were midnight black, framing the stabbing violet of her eyes. "I guess that means I've never lived before today, either."

Autumn was Maxie's favorite time of year. Everything about autumn was more vivid, more breathtaking than any other season. And the fact that the brilliant fall colors lasted such a brief time before the white and gray of winter settled in only made her appreciate autumn more.

Connor drove slowly on his way to nowhere in particlar, windows down and falling leaves occasionally swirling inside the car. He made no attempt to turn on the stereo, which was just fine with Maxie. The sounds of the country seemed particularly rich and soothing, creek water splashing over river rock, tires crunching on dry leaves, a soft background of birdsong and scratching aspen trees. These were sounds alien to city dwellers. When Maxie had first moved back to the country, nature's sounds were as strange to her as a foreign tongue. Crickets had disturbed her sleep, roosters had begun her mornings far too early, the incessant rat-tat-tatting of woodpeckers grated on her raw nerves. She'd heard it all, every little noise. But over time she'd become accustomed, then actually comforted, by Mother Nature's lullaby.

"Listen," she told Connor suddenly. "Listen and tell me what you hear."

He frowned, perplexed. "There's not much to hear, is there? There's a wheat field on the left and a wheat field on the right. As a rule, wheat doesn't make much noise."

Maxie shook her head, frustrated. She wanted to share this with him, she wanted him to understand the healing power of this place she called home. "That's really all you hear?"

"Don't flunk me yet, let me think. I hear your voice, the car's engine...and that pebble that just dinged the windshield. So tell me, what am I supposed to be hearing?"

"That's just it. There's a whole new world of sounds here, but you're not accustomed to listening for them. People who live packed on top of one another in a big city have to concentrate on blocking sounds *out*. Sirens wailing, horns honking, neighbors playing loud music. But here..." she paused, choosing her words carefully, wanting him to understand, "...here there is no such thing as synthetic excitement. No reason to run madly about trying to please strangers. No flash, no dazzle, no glitter. Here everything is real. Here you don't need to guard against anything. You can relax and become a part of the world. It's kind of like sinking to your chin in a delicious, warm bubble bath."

"Now there's a wonderful visual," Connor murmured, a soft smile lighting his eyes. "You, wet skin, bubbles, not too many bubbles, though..."

"I'm trying to educate you," she reminded him, adopting a superior expression despite her faint blush. "Before I moved here, I was always looking around the next corner, wishing for something else. I didn't know what I was looking for, I just knew I didn't have it.''

"The human condition," Connor murmured. "We're always longing for a half-remembered Eden. At least, that's what they say."

"But it doesn't have to be that way." Maxie was bright and earnest as she looked at him, her hand touching his knee for emphasis. "Don't you see? We're meant to be a *part* of nature. We sometimes lose sight of the fact that we need a connection to the world, not insulation from it."

Connor felt a buoyant delight in her sincerity, her childlike enjoyment of this new life. And he was touched this amazing woman wanted to share it with him. "You," he told her, "would make a wonderful missionary. You can go around saving souls, starting with mine."

Maxie stared at him, wondering if he knew the aura he projected—detached, amused but cautious. He reminded her a bit of the person she had been two years earlier. Still, she thought, he was looking for something more. She didn't know why she had come to that conclusion, but somehow she knew. "Tell me something, Connor. Are you happy?"

"Right now?" He glanced sideways, then suddenly pulled the car over to the side of the road, killing the engine. His expression was relaxed, yet Maxie couldn't help but notice the soft heat in his eyes. He half-turned to face her, his arm stretching along the back of the seat. "I'm spending a beautiful afternoon with someone I find absolutely fascinating. She makes me smile. Yes, at this moment I'm happy."

Maxie felt his fingers brush the nape of her neck, and the answering tingle deep in her body. Suddenly the small confines of the car seemed to enclose them with unspoken need. "What about tomorrow?" she asked softly.

"If I worry about tomorrow, I might miss some of today." His index finger traced a slow circle on the nape of her neck. "What about you? Are you happy today, Maxie?"

Maxie bit her lip, her hands smoothing the soft material of her beige jeans. She'd changed before they left, topping the pants with a scoop-necked navy sweater and tying her hair back with a thin navy ribbon. The sweater and jeans were hardly designer clothes, but they fit well, flattering the roundness of her breasts and the curve of her hips. She felt…pretty. Not elegant or sophisticated, not sultry or mysterious. Just pretty.

"Yes," she said softly, raising her gaze to his. "I'm happy today."

Connor was silent for a moment, his dark eyes devouring her features one by one. The compulsion to take her into his arms was so powerful it was almost painful. Still, they were in a small car that left very little room for spontaneity. He contented himself with taking her hand in his own and pressing a butterfly kiss into her upturned palm. She shivered. He ached.

"Picnic," he said with grim determination.

She smiled faintly, nodding her head. "Picnic."

They left the car, jumping a dry irrigation ditch to reach a hillock of young oak trees. The trees still clung to half their leaves, providing a dappled shade perfect for picnicking. Connor carried a small plastic cooler which Maxie assumed contained their mysterious chocolate picnic. He hadn't thought to bring a blanket, but he chivalrously spread his new denim jacket on the ground.

"We'll have to sit close," he apologized, his shining brown eyes as innocent as a cherub's. "I hope you're going to behave yourself."

She cast a humorous glance heavenward. "I will be the soul of propriety," she promised, infusing her voice with an overdose of sincerity.

Connor's only answer to this was a slow smile that curled the edges of his eyes in tiny sunbursts. He tugged on her hair ribbon and told her to sit down. They nestled together, hip against hip. That slight contact was enough to make Connor's heart rate arrhythmic, but he did a masterful job of presenting a calm front. He opened the cooler and pulled out several napkins, carefully smoothing them open on her lap and his like tiny tablecloths. Then he set out his unique offerings, dividing them neatly and evenly: chocolate kisses, chocolate mints, chocolate covered almonds, chocolate truffles and chocolate covered strawberries.

"Oh, this is *wonderful*," Maxie said, clapping her hands as she surveyed the wealth of chocolate on her lap. "No one has ever taken me on a chocolate picnic before. What this meal lacks in nutrition, it more than makes up for with originality. I'm overwhelmed."

"Thank you." He looked absurdly pleased, long legs stretched out before him, the toes of his boots tapping together happily. "Somehow I thought you might like this. If they made chocolate SpaghettiOs, I would have brought them, too."

Maxie shrugged, choosing a huge strawberry with two fingers. "We can't have everything."

"Why not?" Connor said softly. "Who made that rule, we can't have everything?"

"The IRS."

"Funny girl. Fair warning, Maxie. With the exception of a Super Bowl ring, I have a habit of getting everything I want."

Something in his tone made Maxie stare at him, the luscious strawberry on hold two inches from her mouth. There was a heavy-lidded sensuality in his gaze, a look that Maxie couldn't possibly mistake. It seemed to get inside her, to slip beneath her skin and swirl lazily through her body. She felt that look as sure as any touch. "I suppose you do. After all, you got your interview."

"I'm not talking about the interview."

"I am," she said.

Connor noted the breathless quality of her voice with satisfaction. Here he was sharing a cozy picnic with Glitter Baby herself, an astonishing fact he still had trouble getting his mind around. There wasn't a man in the world who wouldn't love to be in his position. Truly, he lived a charmed life, Super Bowl ring or no.

He grinned and took the strawberry from her frozen fingers, popping it into his own mouth. "She who hesitates loses her chocolate. Eat, Maxie. I'll be good."

For once, Maxie seemed to have lost her appetite. She was unusually quiet as she nibbled on her treats, her gaze straying more than once to the man at her side. Sunshine and shade filtered down through the treetops, gilding his hair and broad shoulders with a dozen shades of autumn gold. Replete with chocolate, he leaned back on his elbows and chewed idly on a long blade of grass. The stretch of his lean body was graceful in a powerfully masculine way. The way he smiled whenever their eyes connected made a startling impact on her senses. Oh, that lazy little smile—faint, intoxicating, purely male. Instant bliss.

"You're not eating much," he observed. "Knowing your appetite, I'd say either you were coming down with a terminal illness or you've had too much of a good thing."

*Not enough of a good thing.* "Something like that," she murmured, her eyes straying to the muscular shape of his thighs molded beautifully in soft blue denim. He would have made an absolutely gorgeous cowboy, she thought wistfully.

"Leave the left-overs for the chocolate elves," he suggested, his gaze settling dreamily on her luscious, strawberry stained mouth.

Swallowing hard, Maxie got to her feet and cleared away their picnic with fastidious attention to detail. The napkins and foil wrappers from the chocolate went into the cooler. The remaining chocolate she arranged in a little pile at the base of a tree, an unexpected bounty for the first woodland creature that happened along.

"That ought to make some lucky squirrel very happy," Connor remarked, his eyes unusually bright as he looked up at her. If she didn't know better, she would have sworn he was intoxicated.

"It'll probably kill it," Maxie babbled, looking around for something else to clean up. His unwavering gaze was doing terrible things to her composure. "I have no idea if their little systems can tolerate—"

"I'm through," Connor interrupted in a no nonsense voice.

She looked down at him warily. "Through with what?"

"Being good." His hand snaked out, fingers curling around her ankle. "C'mon," he urged, tugging gently. "You're way up there and I'm way down here and that's just too far away. Stop biting your lip, Maxie, you're going to make it bleed."

"This wasn't on the agenda."

"Speak of your own agenda." Smiling, Connor began to walk his fingers upward along the inseam of her jeans. *"Eensy-weensy spider went up the water spout...."*

Maxie couldn't help it. She made a sound between a whimper and a groan and jumped away from the tantalizing eensy-weensy spider. When it came to the battle of the sexes, this man was armed with a wealth of ammunition. He was funny. He was earnest. He was terribly easy on the eyes. He raised the temperature in her body just by smiling.

"I don't know why I let you do this to me," she muttered, pacing around him in a wide circle. She folded her arms, stuck out her bottom lip and tried to reason with herself. "I've gotten rusty, I guess. Things like this didn't bother me before."

"Things like this?" His golden-brown eyes were dancing a merry jig. "Eating chocolate? Sitting on the ground? Feeding squirrels?"

Maxie blew out a frustrated breath. "You're a hoot. Truly, the most entertaining man. I *meant* things like...you."

"That's ridiculous. I'll have you know I've been on my best behavior several times since I met you."

"Never mind. Just...forget it."

"I will not forget it. Do all men bother you?"

"Of course not."

This seemed to please him to no end. "Really? Then it's just me who bothers you?"

She bristled. "Don't flatter yourself. It's not about you, it's about me. I haven't been alone with a man for two years, that's all. I'm a little...out of practice."

Connor held her eyes for what seemed to be the longest time, the faintest traces of a smile lingering on his mouth. Then he flicked aside his blade of grass and stood up, taking quite a bit of time to tuck the back of his shirt into his jeans. "What you're saying then, is that your reactions to me have nothing to do with me."

Maxie brightened. "That's right. That's *exactly* right."

"The eternal mysteries of feminine logic," he murmured, shaking his head. He picked up his denim jacket from the ground, shook it off and tossed it over a nearby branch. "You know, I'm not an egomaniac. I certainly don't expect you to be attracted to me simply because I'm incredibly attracted to you."

"I wasn't implying—"

"After all, you're the celebrity here." He sauntered towards her, thumbs hooked in the pockets of his jeans. "Have you ever considered how daunting it would be for a man to pursue a relationship with a woman who has fan clubs?"

"*Had* fan clubs."

"Whatever. The whole idea is absolutely terrifying."

He didn't look terrified, Maxie thought, studying him with narrowed eyes. He looked amused, confident and...much too close. She retreated one step at a time until she was brought up short by a tree trunk at her back. She felt trapped in more ways than one, but maintained a calm front. Barely. "Fortunately, you're not pursuing a relationship. You're pursuing an interview, aren't you?"

The toes of his cowboy boots kissed the toes of her leather slipons. "Nah. The fact I landed the interview is just a bonus."

"Really." She cleared her throat. "You're crowding me."

"Actually, I think I'm pursuing you." Connor's smile teased as he placed his palms on the tree trunk on either side of her shoulders. "In fact, I'm almost sure of it."

"Well, you're pursuing me right into this tree." Maxie's respiration quickened as he leaned forward far enough to rest his forehead against hers. She put her hands on his chest with the noble intention of pushing him away. Instead, her rebellious fingers splayed open over his shirt, her palms absorbing heat from his body beneath. "I'll have you know I'm getting thorns in my rear end."

"The scourge of a country picnic, the dreaded aspen tree thorns." He chuckled softly, dropping a delicate kiss on the end of her nose. "You're absolutely adorable when you're cornered. Maxie, do you know how many celebrities I've interviewed in the past few years?"

"No." The single word came out in a nervous falsetto.

"Hundreds. And do you know what makes you different from all these people?"

Something in his warm-brandy eyes sent prickles sparkling along her spine. "No. What?"

"This." His mouth dipped to hers before she could react, his lips dragging over hers with a gentle rocking pressure. His kiss was warm, silken, moist, soft...so many sensations she could hardly identify them all. A sparkling sweetness rippled to the depths of her body, stunning with its pure intensity. His breath swirled with hers, his tongue ever so lightly urging her lips to a willing openness. Maxie's hands turned traitor, closing tightly over fistfuls of his shirt and holding on for dear life. She hadn't been kissed in...oh, so very long. And never, ever like this. She felt his fingers in her hair, stroking the long dark strands, angling her head to deepen the kiss. Like a puppet, she answered to every pull of invisible strings, opening her lips, wanting this man who had been a stranger not two days before. She felt enclosed in a cocoon of luscious warmth, her breasts pressed against his chest, her body straining against the welcoming curve of his hips. His mouth left her lips to leisurely explore her chin, her neck, his tongue tracing a soft, slow circle in the hollow of her throat. A shudder ran through her, hard and deep. Her lips felt like a peach in the summer sun, ripe and swollen with heat and sugar. Connor slowly drew back his head to stare at her with heavy-lidded, passion-drugged eyes. He touched the curve of her shining bottom lip with one shaking finger, a line of fierce intensity etched between his brows.

"Boy meets girl," he whispered. "And suddenly...the whole world is different. Maxie..."

"What?"

He looked blank for a second, then his eyes softened with self-deprecating humor. "I don't know what I was going to say. Just...Maxie."

This time his lips were curled with a smile when he came back to her, smiling when he pressed kisses on each side of her mouth, smiling when he brushed the hair back from her face and kissed her closed eyelids, one at a time. "You're exquisite," he said, cradling her face in his palms and staring at her with more intensity than any photographer had ever shown. "Your skin tastes like roses. And that mouth...that fallen angel mouth of yours has been driving me quietly out of my mind."

"You're never quiet," Maxie gasped, her head dipping back weakly as he explored the baby-soft skin behind her ear with his lips. "Connor..."

His hands went exploring, slipping to the straining fullness of her breasts. Instantly the nipples hardened beneath his fingers, and it was all he could do to keep his touch gentle and undemanding. There was a fierceness building in his chest, a hungry fire pooling in his loins. He felt drugged, as if he were experimenting with an unknown substance that was terribly powerful. "What?"

"That's all. Just...Connor." She held on to his shoulders like a lifeline, willing her knees not to give out on her. "Just...you. I like saying your name. I like the way your eyes smile. The people I used to know...they never smiled with their eyes. You could never trust their smiles."

There was an undercurrent of loneliness in those

words, giving Connor a glimpse of the life she had led for too many years at too young an age. He knew the world of the rich and famous. He'd been born into it, more or less, fully educated and prepared by the sophisticated attitudes of his own parents. But a fourteen-year-old from Wyoming? Dear Lord, little Frances Maxine Calhoon never stood a chance. Eventually she'd managed to escape from that world, but not without her scars. Strange when you considered she had been the envy of nearly every young girl in America. What a terrible difference there was between perception and reality.

He closed his eyes, hating the knowledge that such a tender person had been so hurt.

"What's wrong?" Maxie asked softly.

He pulled back slightly, wondering what sort of expression was on his face. He didn't want to scare her. Hell, he didn't want to scare himself, but the emotions he felt were very real. Every cell in his body was alive and aching for her. This was need on a new level, a level he had no experience with. Need to protect her, need to soothe and cheer and gratify her. No matter how close he held her, he didn't think he would ever be close enough.

"Nothing's wrong, beautiful girl." He kissed her parted lips one last, lingering time. "Except I don't know how to let you go."

Maxie reached up a shaking hand to thread her fingers dreamily through his tumbled hair. "Then we're going to get awfully cold once the sun goes down."

His dazzling smile accepted the challenge. "I could keep you warm."

"Oh, I'll just bet you could," she said softly. She

kissed him lightly on his strong jaw, then quickly ducked beneath his suddenly empty arms. "We need to leave now, Mr. Garrett."

He turned, the set of his lips suspiciously similar to a pout. "And why do we have to leave now?"

She looked over her shoulder and smiled at him, her violet eyes flirting outrageously as she continued walking slowly backwards to the car. "Because," she purred softly, "I don't want to."

She took off running, leaving the former football quarterback in the dust.

# Six

Maxie had spent eight long years pretending to be someone she wasn't. She had posed just the way she was told, walked in a certain way, dressed as people expected her to dress. She had been an invention of others, clothed, painted and sprayed to suit whichever client she was working for, whichever product she was endorsing. No one admired the woman beneath the mask, because no one had been interested in getting to know the woman beneath the mask.

Then Connor Garrett had found his way to her.

Initially he had set out searching for Glitter Baby, but the woman he'd found was Maxie Calhoon—flaws, fertilizer and all. Lord knew there was no mysterious aura surrounding her these days. Still, unless she was much mistaken, Connor seemed to prefer the reality to the myth. She was still cautious, naturally, but it was getting harder to deny the curious lightness in her heart, the feeling of delicious anticipation.

She looked sideways at him as they drove back to the ranch, noting the bands of flushed color still on his cheekbones. His profile was quite perfect, almost as good as a full face shot. She played those words back in her mind and started to laugh. Definitely too many years spent in front of the cameras.

"Did I miss something?" Connor asked curiously.

"No." Maxie smiled, shaking her head. "Sorry, I was just preoccupied with…something."

He cleared his throat. "Why do you keep looking at me? You're making me self-conscious."

Maxie shrugged, deliberately turning her head toward the window to hide her smile. "So who made the rule that says women can't look at men? You make a darn cute cowboy."

"Oh hell, please don't start that again."

"Sorry." Then, with a giggle, "Did you know you blush around the ears when you're embarrassed? It's the most amazing thing I've ever seen."

He bristled. "The hell you say."

"I'm sorry, I'm sorry." Still laughing, Maxie tipped her head back on the seat. It had turned out, she decided, to be the most wonderful afternoon. Even now her body felt pleasantly heavy, unfamiliar and ripe with lingering desire. How strange it all felt, this burgeoning physical and spiritual connection with another human being. She'd spent so much time insulating herself against just that.

She wondered if she ought to ask him to stay for dinner. She didn't want to seem too eager, yet neither was she ready to say goodbye. The soft, lingering euphoria surrounding her was still tickling her, playing with her senses. It was intoxicating, and if she had the antidote to this sweet poison, she would probably toss it out the window. It was far more interesting, she decided, to sit back, relax and wait for whatever happened next.

And what happened next turned out to be a surprise for both of them.

Still hot around the ears, Connor turned down the dirt road leading to her ranch house. He'd told himself all the way home he wasn't going to make a pest of himself and ask to come in. If he pushed too hard, she might be scared off. He'd made quite a bit of progress, and didn't want to ruin things by being too demanding. It was so important he did this right. He'd never experienced this intense fascination with a woman. Everything Maxie said, everything she felt was important to him. She didn't know how she looked to him today, sun-flushed and natural, her wonderful eyes sparkling with simple happiness. Oh, those eyes…they were a mirror for every thought she had.

"So what are you doing tonight?" he asked, trying and failing to sound casual. "Any plans?"

"Oh, you know, pretty much what I do every night. Chores and…stuff." *Do I ask him to stay for dinner?*

"I had a good time today. I hate to see it end." *How obvious can I be?*

"So did I," Maxie said softly, meeting his bright, coaxing eyes. "I never said thank-you for the chocolate picnic, did I? You went to a lot of trouble for—" She stopped, brought up short by the beige Toyota parked in front of her house. "My mother," she ended lamely.

Connor shook his head, wondering what he'd missed. "Your mother? You think I went to a lot of trouble for your mother?"

"No, I just meant..." Maxie gulped, pointing at the cheerfully smiling woman waving from the front porch. In her neon-orange sweater, she stood out like a flagman on the highway. "That's my mother."

In Connor's worst nightmares, he had not anticipated meeting Maxie's mother while his body was still tense with passion and the only thought in his head was getting Maxie back in his arms. "How nice," he said. "There she is, standing on the porch."

"There she is," Maxie repeated, glancing in the rearview mirror. Her swollen lips looked thoroughly kissed, her eyes heavy-lidded and her cheeks blazed like poppies. "Well...would you like to come inside and meet her?"

It was the invitation he had hoped for, but not precisely the circumstances he'd anticipated. "I was hoping you'd ask."

Natalie was so pleased, she could hardly contain herself.

She was seeing a side to her daughter that absolutely delighted her. She'd wondered how long it would take for Maxie to heal from her scars, how long it would be before her isolation became more lonely than comforting. She wanted nothing more than for her daughter to lead a normal life, particularly since she would always feel responsible for allowing Maxie to undertake a modeling career at such a young age in the first place.

"So, the two of you had a picnic," Natalie said

to Connor. She was sitting in the recliner while Connor had taken the sofa. Obviously he wasn't relaxed. His hands were folded prayerlike in his lap and his posture was painfully erect. She wondered impishly if he realized he had grass stains on his knees and a leaf tangled in his hair. "I can't tell you how delighted I am. I've always thought Maxie should get out more. And with this Indian summer weather, you had a nice, warm day for your outing."

"Very warm." Connor glanced longingly at the front door. Maxie had changed her clothes and gone outside to see to the cows nearly thirty minutes earlier. How long did it take to see to the cows? "Your daughter is wonderful company, Mrs. Calhoon."

"Call me Natalie. Maxie told me how she met you, Connor. Your tenacity is impressive. No one has been able to track her down for more than two years."

"I want you to know something," Connor said quietly. "I met her initially because I wanted to interview Glitter Baby. But the woman I've come to know, the woman I spent time with today is Maxie Calhoon. She is a remarkable woman."

Natalie smiled faintly. "I've always known that. And believe me, Maxie wouldn't be spending time with you if she felt your interest in her was anything but genuine. She learned quite a bit living out there among the wolves."

"You seem quite happy her career is over."

"Happier than I can tell you. Maxie's father was not an easy man to live with. I was afraid Maxie would never know what self-esteem was unless she was allowed to leave. Needless to say, that turned out to be a terrible mistake on my part." A shadow crossed her features. "She nearly didn't survive. When she finally came home, she was a fragile wisp of a thing. It took her forever just to learn to eat and sleep again. I blame myself for that."

"You must be very proud of her now," Connor said gently. "She seems to love this life she's made for herself."

Natalie nodded, brightening. "She does. I've never seen her so happy. I would hate to see anything mar that."

They understood one another. Connor told her as much with his faint smile. "That makes two of us, Natalie. I would never allow anyone or anything to hurt your daughter."

Natalie was quiet for a long moment. Then, choosing her words carefully, said, "I'm sure you wouldn't hurt her intentionally. What you may not realize about my daughter is that she's still quite naïve, quite vulnerable. Maxie never went to a high-school prom, never went off to college, never even had a serious boyfriend. She missed all that. When other girls were shopping for a prom dress, Maxie was working the Paris fashion shows. She never went to the mall with her friends, never had a teenage crush, never went to high-school football games. All those experiences—and the emotional maturity that comes with them—Maxie missed out on. Photographs of her show the most polished celebrity you can imagine. The reality is quite the opposite."

Natalie watched him digest her insights with great interest. Usually she was a good judge of character, and Connor Garrett struck her as being a sincere and caring man. Still, one couldn't be too careful. Her daughter was a very special human being, and it was obvious Connor had found a way beneath her defenses.

Their gazes met, then Connor looked down at his clasped hands. "Are you asking if my intentions are honorable?"

Natalie laughed, a husky, delicious sound that reminded Connor forcibly of Maxie. "No, no. I just wanted to tell you be careful with her. She's unlike anyone you've ever met, Connor. When Maxie finally gives her heart, it will be for the first and last time in her life."

He smiled, liking Natalie's direct attitude. "You're very much like your daughter, do you realize that? No smoke screens, no pretenses. I admire that. I don't know many people in this world who practice unvarnished honesty."

"It's a lost art," Natalie acknowledged, a mischievous sparkle in her eyes. "It can also annoy other people tremendously, which is why I would advise not telling Maxie about our little talk."

Connor grinned, imagining what Maxie would do had she been eavesdropping on their conversation. "I value my life, Natalie. It's not much, but it's mine own. I can safely promise you I won't tell Maxie a thing."

"Lovely. That's the kind of unvarnished honesty I like."

They were still laughing when Maxie walked in the door. "And here I worried the two of you might be feeling uncomfortable," she said, looking curiously from her mother to Connor and back again. "Being strangers and all. Mother, what have you done?"

"Nothing," Natalie said indignantly. "Surely you

don't think me incapable of carrying on a polite conversation?''

''How rude,'' Connor put in mildly. ''Your mother has been very gracious.''

''What were you laughing at?'' Maxie persisted.

''I told a knock-knock joke,'' Natalie explained. She stood up, giving her daughter a brief hug. ''Darling, I have to run. It's been lovely seeing you.''

''But you haven't seen me,'' Maxie said, bewildered. ''At least stay for dinner—''

''I really can't, sweetie. Next time.'' She gave Connor a bright smile over her shoulder. ''Goodbye. It was lovely meeting you. And thank you for laughing at all my jokes.''

''No,'' Connor said quietly. He stood up, offering Natalie his hand. ''Thank *you*.''

Maxie closed the door behind her mother, then turned and gave Connor a look that said she wasn't fooled a bit. ''I know my mother,'' she announced. ''She does *not* tell knock-knock jokes.''

Connor shrugged. ''Oh, but she does. She should do standup comedy. Her delivery is excellent. How were the cows?''

''Very well, thank you for asking.'' Maxie gave him a sugar-sweet smile as she pulled off her rubber boots. ''I love a good joke, Connor. Tell me.''

He looked at her blankly. ''Tell you…?''

''My mother's joke. I'll refresh your memory. Knock-knock…''

''My lamentable memory,'' he sighed. ''Forgive me, I'm just a poor, dumb football player…at least I was. Have I ever told you how fetching you look in overalls?''

Maxie immediately assumed a sultry expression,

planted her hands on her hips and "walked the walk." Six steps forward, half turn, pause, six steps back. "The latest in prestained overalls," she intoned haughtily. "A must for the style-conscious milk-maid."

Connor's smile was slow, sexy and a little wicked around the edges. Even when she was parodying herself, she raised the temperature in the room by twenty degrees. "Only you could make a pair of overalls appealing, Frances Maxine. C'mere."

She shook her head, laughing. "I smell like a Holstein. If you'll give me a minute to shower, I'll fix you something for dinner. What do you feel like?"

He caught her eyes and held them. "Do you really want me to answer that?"

"I don't know what the world is like where you come from, mister, but around here we treat milk-maids with respect." Maxie giggled, giving him a wide berth as she walked towards the bedroom. "Give me ten minutes to clean up. And then, cowboy, I've got a real treat for you. Just how much do you know about old-fashioned western hospitality?"

Connor looked hopeful. "I've heard rumors."

Maxie wiggled her eyebrows at him, her smile luminous. "They're all true. Just you wait and see."

"That's not how you spell *lingerie*."

"Of course it is," Connor replied.

"You left an *i* out, between the *r* and the *e*."

"When did they start spelling it like that?"

"Connor, if you want to look it up—"

"Okay, fine. I have a wide and varied vocabulary. I can come up with another word. Give me a minute."

They were stretched out on their stomachs on the living-room floor, a Scrabble board between them. Maxie's elbows were on the carpet, her chin resting in her hands. She was chewing on her lower lip, mostly trying to control her smile.

"Western hospitality," Connor grumbled. "I fell for that one big time. Who the hell plays Scrabble anymore? Wait…wait, wait. I have one." He rearranged the letters and looked up at her with a triumphant smile. "Ha! How's that for creativity?"

Maxie looked at the board. *"Lechery?"*

*"Lechery,"* he confirmed. "That gives me a total of…forty-eight points. Your turn."

"You should be in therapy, Connor." Maxie arranged her letters on the board with careful precision. "There you go."

Connor cocked one eyebrow. *"Repent?"*

She assumed an angelic expression. "It means—"

"I know what it means," Connor interrupted. He was having a devil of a time keeping his mind on the game. Maxie had come from her shower smelling of apple-blossom shampoo and dressed in faded jeans and a scoop-necked white T-shirt. It was a modest enough outfit for sitting at the kitchen table and eating tuna sandwiches, but modesty flew out the window when she'd stretched out on the carpet across from him. There was just no way to ignore the luscious cleavage across the old Scrabble board.

But he'd tried for almost thirty minutes now. And thirty minutes, he suddenly decided, was more than enough.

"Oh, dear." He swept his arm across the board, clearing it of every single letter. "Look what I've gone and done. I guess that's the end of the game."

Maxie raised her eyelids slowly, gazing at him through a sultry screen of black lashes. "Hmmm. I take it you don't want to play games."

The expression on her face left Connor struggling for air. She was a delicious mixture of child and woman, a barefoot temptress with still damp clouds of hair, a siren's smile and captivating violet eyes that held a world of secrets.

"You're right, beautiful girl." He lifted a hand, touching the dark silk of her hair. "When you play a game, someone has to win and someone has to lose. Those are bad odds, I've decided."

Maxie let out her breath in a soft sigh as he slowly traced the outline of her parted lips with his finger. "What are you doing?"

"I'm not playing games." He gave her a smile, such a smile as the loyal viewers of *Public Eye* had never seen. It could have baked bread at ten paces.

"You and your smile," Maxie managed breathlessly, "shouldn't be let out after dark. You're a menace to virtuous women."

"Really?" He looked positively delighted. "I only wish to be a menace to one woman."

Maxie considered this, her mouth quirked at one corner. Then, with a deep breath that did wondrous things to her T-shirt, she said, "Okay. Menace away, please."

Connor had been a favorite of the ladies since puberty. He had enough experience to handle himself pretty well in your normal man-woman situation. But never, *ever* had he been face-to-face with a beautiful woman who happily gave him permission to "menace away," then stared at him with eager anticipation. It put a crimp in his style.

"Maxie, how am I supposed to…I mean, I would appreciate it if we could just take things…oh, to hell with it."

His years of football training stood him in good stead. With one graceful maneuver, he had Maxie on her back, both of her hands caught in his above her head. He went down to her mouth like a starving man, lips fastening hungrily over hers. He felt as if it had been years, ages, eons since he'd kissed her. Oh, those swollen, sinful lips…they seemed to brand him with her own unique variety of liquid fire. His tongue tasted hers and he shuddered clear through to his soul. This was like kissing a flower, still damp with morning dew. He drank deeply, slanting his head this way and that to get the full measure of her, yet still he couldn't get enough.

When he finally lifted his head, his eyes were heavy-lidded and glazed with sexual heat. He gazed down at her, touching her cheek with shaking fingers. "You look like an angel," he whispered, "who has just been thoroughly kissed."

The faintest hint of a smile touched her pouty lips. "I don't feel like an angel. I feel…*menaced.*"

"Tell me something," Connor murmured. "How do you like to be kissed? Gently…like this…" He covered her lips ever-so-softly with a kiss as light as butterfly wings. "Or do you like it a little wicked…like this…" Again he took her lips in a long, demanding kiss, graphic and uncontrolled. The contrast between the two was powerfully erotic. Maxie's hips began to stir fitfully against his, pushing, rocking, aching.

"That's not *so* wicked," she gasped, clinging to his shoulders with both hands. "I can handle it."

"I'm not done, child." His mouth kissed a smile against her petal-soft neck. "Have you always been so impatient?"

Maxie moaned as she felt her breasts settle into his seeking hands. His tongue traced tiny little circles over the pulse at her throat, then drifted lower, closing over the soft fabric of her T-shirt to suckle her nipples. The cool wetness through the light fabric was a shock, sending hot-cold sparks along her nerve endings. He suckled her long and slow, reducing her to a state of mute ecstasy. The gentle tug of his lips seemed to pull at the very heart of her. She gasped out a small sob when he finally pushed the fabric of her shirt above her breasts. She thought she might die from the pleasurable rush of air on her damp nipples. And, she thought hazily, it would be a splendid way to go.

"Am I hurting you?" He lifted his head, his eyes the darkest brown beneath a silken tangle of dishevelled hair. "Maxie?"

"Don't want to talk," she murmured. Her hands moved hungrily over his shoulders, kneading ridges of tensed, rock-hard muscles. Then they roved lower, exploring the gentle hollow of his back and the strong rise of his buttocks. "Your body is wonderful. You feel so…so…uhmmm…what are you doing?"

He held her eyes, deliberately moving against her with an age-old rhythm. She held his, reaching down to touch the damp, rock-hard nipples he had made such beautiful love to. It was an instinctive, purely sensual move Connor hadn't expected from her, nor was he prepared for what it did to him to watch her touch herself. The resulting shock waves in his body came close to ending the whole thing right there.

Never in his life had he been so completely out of control. And their clothes were still on.

Connor stilled his movements, willing himself not to explode. "Slowing down would be a good idea," he managed hoarsely, eyes closed tight as he frantically tried to locate his willpower.

"Why?" Maxie's soft voice seemed to come from far away. "Did I do something wrong?"

"No, you did not do..." His eyes opened slowly, pupils wide and distended as he stared at the beautiful, rose-flushed face beneath him. Something Maxie's mother had said to him earlier came back with a vengeance. *When she finally gives her heart, it will be for the first and last time in her life.*

"Maxie? This is probably a stupid question, but, when you asked if you'd done something wrong..."

A wary look came into her eyes. "What about it?"

"You almost sounded like you've never...you've never actually..."

Maxie pulled a deep, sustaining breath into her lungs. She was trapped, well and truly trapped. How embarrassing, considering her scandalous, wild-child reputation.

"Hard to believe, isn't it?" she said glumly. "Twenty-four years old and still...extremely well-preserved."

Connor gaped. He couldn't see his own expression, but somehow he knew he was gaping. It simply had never occurred to him that Maxie might be a virgin. Never. And considering her impassioned and uninhibited response to him, it was even harder to believe.

He rolled over on his back, lying shoulder to shoulder with her while he waited for his rational thought process to kick in. "I'm a little confused," he said finally.

She blushed painfully. "I'm sorry. Maybe I should have said something. I'm not exactly sure of the etiquette here. Particularly when you consider my somewhat notorious background. Lack of trust was always a problem for me. I knew darn well no one wanted Frances Maxine Calhoon. Glitter Baby was the big draw. My pride just wouldn't let me...well, anyway, there you have it. I'm sorry."

His hand found hers, closing tight. "Hell, don't be sorry. Maxie, if I had known...if I had even *suspected*...well, I'd have been a little more attentive to the details, to put it mildly."

At his statement she glanced sideways, clearly impressed. "Really? You can do what you did with even *more* attention to the details?"

"I can certainly try," Connor muttered. "Maxie, when it happens between us—and make no mistake, it will happen—it's not going to be on the living-room floor after a rousing game of Scrabble. I got a little carried away there for a minute, but it won't happen again."

"It won't?"

The woeful look on her face made Connor smile. "Let me put it another way," he said huskily. "Someday in the future when you think back on the first time, I want you to have absolutely no regrets."

"Of all the damn things," she muttered. Then, though she could hardly think of a reason why, she started laughing. Not a mere chuckle, either, but a good, hard belly laugh. At first Connor looked at her the same way he'd looked at Harvey, the lop-eared rabbit—completely befuddled. Then he started to laugh as well, carried away by the absurdity of their situation. They laughed until there was no breath left, until their sides were splitting and their eyes were streaming.

When Maxie could finally find her breath, she said, "It's not funny. Here I am, a *retiree,* no less, with my virginity still hanging like a millstone around my neck. No one would believe it, either."

"I really don't give a damn what anyone else thinks." Connor sat up, drawing his legs to his chest and resting his forehead on his knees. Then, in a muffled voice, "Except you. I care terribly what you think. Maxie?"

"What?"

He lifted his head, looking down at her with a strange smile. "Is that all right with you? If I care terribly?"

She nodded slowly, her body still feeling fragile and unfamiliar. "It would make us even," she whispered.

She thought he might kiss her again then, but he didn't. Drawing on the last of his resolve, he stood, held out his hand and pulled her to her feet. As soon as she was steadied, he let go, shoving his hands in his pockets.

"I hear a cold shower calling my name," he said, striving for a lighter note. "I'll call you later, all right?"

"You don't have to go."

"Yes, I do, sweetheart. I happen to have very little willpower where you're concerned." And still he stood there, staring at her over-bright eyes, her passion-stained cheeks, the way her bare toes dug self-consciously into the carpet. She was perfect. She was everything he had never known he needed, till now. He smiled at her with such tenderness that tears misted her eyes. Then he turned and left without another word.

# Seven

As Connor drove through the darkened countryside, he replayed every moment he had spent with Maxie since that first day at the feed store. When that wasn't enough, he picked up his cell phone and called her number.

She picked up halfway through the second ring. "Hello?"

"It's me." He paused, listening. "Is that water running?"

"I'm in the bath." There was rueful amusement in her voice. "Some people take cold showers, some take warm baths."

"I wish I hadn't heard that," he muttered. "I'm not sure why I called. I think I miss your voice. Have I ever told you how sexy your voice is? It always sounds a little hoarse, like you have a cold. It's really cute."

"Connor, are you all right?"

"Sure. Just a little separation anxiety. Anyway, be careful. Don't use your blow dryer or your electric toothbrush while you're in there." Why the *hell* had he said that? Connor winced and let go of the steering wheel long enough to thump himself on the forehead with the heel of his hand. His reputation as a smooth operator was obviously a thing of the past. Maxie affected him as no other woman ever had. He was a stranger to himself. "I'm going to hang up now. I need to get my foot out of my mouth."

He was still rolling his eyes at his own idiocy when he turned down Main Street. Things were hopping in Oakley on this particular Friday night. The Dairy Queen was packed. Trucks and cars cruised up and down the wide, two-lane street, horns honking and teenagers calling out to one another. There was even a line—six people—waiting in front of the ticket office at the Westwind Theater. *The Parent Trap* was playing this evening, the original version with Hayley Mills. Connor felt like he had fallen through some cosmic black hole back into the fifties.

He drove past the small brick high school, reading the marquee with amusement. Lady Redskins Basketball Tryouts Monday. And below that, in big block letters, HOMECOMING DANCE SATURDAY!

Connor's smile started way down in his chest and spread like sunlight to his eyes and lips. Again he picked up the phone and punched redial.

"Hello?" She sounded breathless.

"Me, again. Still in the tub?"

"No. I'm toweling off."

"Oh, boy." Connor closed his eyes briefly to appreciate the picture. "You don't make this very easy, do you? Maxie, this time I'm calling for a good reason. Will you please go out with me tomorrow night?''

''You called back to ask me for a date?''

''Yeah. My dad said I could have the car.''

She started laughing and it was by far the sweetest sound Connor Garrett had ever heard.

''I'd love to,'' she said.

The first package arrived just before noon the following day. Maxie's face was blue at the time. When the delivery man tapped on the door, she happened to be marinating beneath a mud mask, using the last of an obscenely expensive concoction left over from her obscenely indulgent modeling days. She was primping for her date.

She pulled the door open a crack. ''Yes?''

The man smiled, then jumped back in alarm. ''Good hell...I mean, good morning, ma'am. I have a package for you. If I could have your signature?''

Maxie signed. He fled. She took the package to the kitchen and sat down at the table to open it. She gasped as lavender satin spilled out of the box like a lustrous bouquet of flowers. It was a sleeveless, floor-length dress, exquisite in its utter simplicity. Maxie knew with a certainty it had not been purchased in Oakley, Wyoming. The card inside was not signed, but it didn't need to be. ''Wear this tonight,'' was all the card said.

The shoes were delivered an hour later, strappy silver sandals that were almost invisible. She had no idea how Connor knew her size, but they fitted perfectly. Again, she doubted very much they came from the discount shoe store in town.

The final package was delivered an hour before Connor was supposed to pick her up. Inside was a delicate silver choker, so fragile it looked spun out of silver threads.

Maxie wondered if Connor knew there was really no place to go within fifty miles with a formal dress code. Regardless, it was actually a pleasure to spend a good part of the afternoon on such frivolous activities as hairstyling and makeup. It had been so long since she'd indulged herself like this. When looking good ceased to be a job, it was actually a treat. She only hoped Connor would recognize her without the overalls.

The doorbell rang at precisely seven o'clock. Maxie took one last look at her reflection in the mirror, fortified herself with a deep breath and went to let him in.

"Well, look at you, Frances Maxine." Connor's dark eyes were wider and brighter than she had ever seen. His stunned gaze traveled from the top of her head to the tips of her toes. He placed his hand over his heart, as if to encourage it to continue beating. "You're...you're..."

She looked down at her dress, chewing on her lower lip. "I'm...what?"

"I can't describe it." Connor walked slowly inside, shutting the door behind him with his foot. His busy eyes were on their third head-to-toe trip. "You look more beautiful than any photograph that was ever taken of you. Your hair...and that dress..."

She smiled self-consciously, at the same time taking in the picture he made in a black tuxedo. He wore it with easy confidence, the pristine white shirt a dazzling contrast against his dark skin. His glossy, honey-colored hair appeared to have been trimmed, shorter at the sides, waving over his collar in the back. His heavy-lidded brown eyes had never looked so warm and appealing.

"You clean up pretty well," she said in a massive understatement. "They're going to love you at the bowling alley."

"What bowling alley?" The corners of his mouth tucked in a curious smile. "You think we're going bowling?"

"As near as I can figure, the bowling alley is the only place in town open late on Saturday night." But Connor only chuckled, apparently deciding not to explain. For the first time, Maxie noticed the small plastic container Connor carried. "What's that?"

"Oh. I forgot all about it, what with the stunning scenery." He opened the box, then placed a white gardenia corsage on Maxie's wrist. "There. I thought I should get you the kind of corsage you pin on your dress, but the lady at Gretta's Floral said everyone else ordered wrist corsages."

"Everyone else? Everyone else who?"

"You're very inquisitive tonight," Connor reproved, his eyes sparkling wickedly. "On the plus side, you're so beautiful it breaks my heart just to look at you."

"I didn't thank you for my presents, did I?" She smoothed the material of her gown with gentle fingers. "You have wonderful taste. How on earth did you know the size?"

"I have my sources."

"Well, thank you. I haven't felt like this for…oh, longer than I could say."

"Neither have I," Connor said softly, talking

about something else altogether. "And it just keeps getting better. Are you ready to go?"

"I refuse to leave until you tell me where we're going."

"Okay," he said easily. "I'll go alone, then."

"You're so stubborn." Maxie pulled a face as he turned to the door. "Fine. I'm right behind you."

He opened the door, then stepped back to usher her outside. "I'd rather have you in front of me. The view is much better."

By the time he pulled into the high-school parking lot, Connor was wondering if this was such a hot idea, after all. Glitter Baby was sitting beside him, the woman who had been everywhere and knew everyone. This was the woman who had twice been featured on the cover of *People* magazine as one of the most beautiful faces in the world. And where was Connor Garrett taking her on their first, all-important official date?

Oakley High School homecoming dance.

Anxiously he watched her looking around the parking lot, held his breath as her eyes went to the homecoming dance announcement on the marquee. "Cat's out of the bag," he said, attempting a light note that fell rather flat. "Look, there really is a method to my madness. When I was talking to your mother yesterday, she mentioned you'd never had a chance to go to a high-school dance. I just thought you might like to find out what you missed."

"Connor—"

"I know it's weird, especially for someone who's been all over the world, but—"

She turned and kissed him softly on the cheek, a

kiss that felt like a benediction. When he looked down at her face, it was like seeing a beautiful vision: clouds of dark hair, violet eyes swimming in tears and the dusky, wet-cinnamon lips that constantly paralyzed his thought processes.

"No one has ever done anything like this for me in my entire life," she said, smiling and wiping a tear off her cheek.

Connor still wasn't quite sure if this was a good thing or a bad thing. "So...it's all right?"

"You have no idea how all right it is," she whispered. She was conscious of a new feeling stirring to life within her, something sweet and innocent and hopeful. No man had ever spoken to her in this language before, the language of the heart. No one had ever tried.

Connor finally relaxed then, knowing she understood. Tonight was about lost childhood wishes and half-forgotten dreams. More than anything in the world, he wanted to make hers come true. Just to see that light of wonder in her eyes made it all worthwhile for him.

"C'mon, Cinderella," he said, clearing his throat to cover a tremor of emotion in his voice. "You're going to the ball."

Maxie had often wondered what a high-school dance would have been like. Now she knew, although she suspected she was enjoying the event far more than she ever would have in high school. The dance was held in the school gymnasium, the ceiling thick with balloons and dangling crepe-paper streamers. Pink dresses were abundant, as were carnation wrist corsages. Maxie and Connor were the object of many quizzical glances, but for once the attention didn't bother her a bit. Most of the fresh-faced students attending the dance would have still been in grade school throughout much of her Glitter Baby heyday. Chances are, Maxie told herself, they'd never even heard of her. How absolutely wonderful.

They danced each and every dance, enjoyed cookies and punch—definitely *not* spiked, Connor pronounced with disappointment—and danced again. Later, Maxie couldn't remember what sort of music the DJ played, but she remembered the scent of Connor's cologne when her face was nestled against his chest. She remembered the way he had laughed when they'd gone outside for fresh air and a gust of wind had billowed beneath her skirt, coming very close to making her a centerfold. And when his laughter had subsided, he had pulled her around the corner of the building to a secluded spot and kissed her frantically until she had lost her breath entirely.

When the final strains of the last dance faded away, it was precisely midnight. Connor looked at his watch, one side of his mouth tipped up in a smile. "Well, little girl? Don't you need to be home by midnight?"

Maxie stared at him for the longest time, quite sure that her heart was in her eyes. "I've had a wonderful time being young again," she said softly. "I can never thank you enough for this night. But now, if you don't mind, I'd like to go home with you and try my hand at being a woman."

Connor seemed unnaturally still. His smile fell off his face by degrees and his breathing became quietly arrhythmic. He truly didn't know how to respond, so the first thought that bounded through his mind, he blurted out. "This never happened to me when I was back in high school."

The whisper of a reckless smile touched her mouth, her eyes soft with passion. "Shameless, aren't I? Come home with me, please."

If he was dreaming, Connor decided, he never wanted to wake up.

# Eight

Maxie's house slept in shadows, the only noise in the hushed darkness sounded like a freight train coming from the corner of the living room.

"That's just Boo," Maxie explained, when Connor stopped short three steps into the room. "He has asthma, so he snores terribly. That's why I make him sleep out here instead of in my room."

Connor made a mental note never to snore again. "He didn't even wake up when we walked in. If he wasn't making so much noise, I'd wonder if he was alive. *This* is your guard dog?"

"It's not his shift," she said. "Harvey's on duty tonight." She flicked on a lamp, then turned and gave him a rather hesitant smile. Swathed in the soft pool of light, she had an ethereal beauty that surrounded him, flooding his senses, his heart, his mind.

"You've been awfully quiet. What are you thinking?"

"I'm trying to believe you really happened to me," he said with gentle sincerity. "Even now I expect to wake up any second."

"Is that what this is with us?" Maxie tilted her head inquisitively. "A dream?"

"It can't be." Connor had taken off his jacket and tie during the ride home. His white shirt was open at the neck with the sleeves rolled up, yet Maxie somehow knew he wasn't as relaxed as he looked. "This is better than any dream I've ever had."

Silence settled between them, thick with soft sensuality. Maxie's gaze was solemn and intense, as if she were tasting him with her eyes. "You look like a little boy," she said thoughtfully. "Your hair is mussed, all soft and tumbled. I like it like that."

"Thank you." He closed the distance between them, taking her face in his hands. "I can tell you with all sincerity that I'm not a little boy, Maxie."

She closed her eyes briefly, rubbing her cheek lovingly against his open palm like a kitten. "Whatever you say, Connor."

"Really?" The look he gave her was shimmering with heat. "*Whatever?*"

She pressed a smile on the pulse at his wrist. "Uh-huh. Whatever. I trust you completely."

He dropped his forehead against hers, his hands sliding up and down her back. He was caught up in her eyes, lost in the clear, stabbing color. Tenderness spiralled within him, a strange urge to both protect and to possess. "I would never hurt you, little love. Never."

"I know that," she said simply. She melted

against him, a soft, erotic weight on his hips and chest. "Do you feel like menacing?"

He shook his head, his cheeks marked with bright bands of passion. "Not tonight."

She pulled back slightly. "No? As in...no?"

He laughed quietly, hearing his own nerves in the sound. "Sweetheart, menacing isn't nearly as fun as what we're about to do."

This seemed to please her. "Really?"

"Really." Connor's smile disappeared as he stared down at her face. Holding her was like holding everything he had ever wanted in his life. His arms slipped around her waist, fingers threaded together at the small of her back. "Maxie Calhoon, the world will never see your like again."

She tipped back her head, her hair drifting to her waist in back. He could feel its cool satin caressing his hands. "I don't care about the world," she whispered helplessly. "I care about you."

Connor kissed her softly, his mouth moving against hers with cool sensuality. Playful. Gentle. Oh, how he loved her beautiful lips. He could never get enough. When the kiss threatened to become wild, he broke away, scooping one arm beneath her thighs and lifting her off her feet. Flushed, aroused, she rode in his arms to the bedroom, pressing a dozen frantic kisses over his face and neck. They sat together on the edge of the mattress at first, not thinking to remove their clothes, but happily exploring with their hands and mouths. They kissed until their breathing was hard and reckless. Then, still holding her lips, Connor fell backward on the bed, pulling her down with him. Maxie was on top of him now, and clothed or not, the position all but obliterated

sanity for Connor. He kissed her with a new, more
desperate intent until her hips were grinding against
him in a sensual frenzy. Her fingers dug into his soft,
tangled hair, her breasts surged against his chest,
every cell in her body yearned towards him.

Connor tried to deepen the kiss even further, slanting his head from side to side, giving more, receiving
more. He could feel her hair swinging against his
face, cooling his hot skin. He could feel her deliberately moving against his hardness, trying to sate
herself in a way she didn't fully understand. Her hunger was the most potent aphrodisiac Connor had ever
known. She wanted him with the same fierce intensity he wanted her. They were starving.

"I have to tell you…" Connor whispered. Maxie
gasped as he kneaded her breasts over lavender satin.
"I'm going to tear this beautiful dress. It wasn't
made for this kind of thing."

Later she couldn't remember Connor unzipping
her dress and letting it fall to the floor. She did remember, however, the way he looked at her in her
bra and panties, and she remembered being the one
who tore them off. Shameless hussy that she was,
she also fumbled at his belt, the buttons on his shirt.
She needed to see all of him, feel all of him. The
sight and sensation were better than she ever could
have imagined. He was tanned, hard and powerfully
muscled. Beautiful, Maxie thought hazily. He was
truly beautiful.

Connor crackled with tension from head to foot.
Every muscle in his body was straining for release.
He'd never known a wanting like this, so sharp and
acute it was almost painful. They rolled together on
the bed, legs tangling, arms reaching, lips seeking.

The only light in the room came from a generous full moon slanting through the windows. It bathed them in cool shadows, illuminating their faces and bodies just enough. Connor took pictures in his mind, keepsakes for all eternity. Maxie, wearing nothing but a silver necklace, her incredible skin gleaming like oiled ivory. Her love-hazed smile, the sparkling moisture on her irresistible lips. Her hair clinging damply to her shoulders, falling over her like a veil. The beautiful shape of her woman's body, the length of her slender throat, her fragile, feminine hands and fingers. There was no hesitation or self-consciousness on her part. She seemed to want it all, every experience and sensation he could give her. And she wanted it with a fervor he had never seen before.

They communicated in half-finished, gasping sentences, too joy-filled to articulate further. The closer they got, the closer they needed to be. Maxie could hardly endure the unfamiliar ache between her legs. It intensified by the second, making her crazy with the desire to find relief.

"I need...I want..." She couldn't finish. She was lost in a dizzying whirlwind. This was an exquisite, glorious pain. *"Help me."*

"I will, sweetheart," Connor rasped, trying to breathe and think and feel all at the same time. He was half out of his mind with desire. Still, he had to think of Maxie. "We can't...I want to be careful with you, protect you. I need to get—"

"No, you don't," Maxie gasped, struggling to think coherently. "I've been taking something for the last two years, just in case...I met someone like you. So...you can...you know."

"Oh, I know," Connor murmured, his mouth finding hers repeatedly. His hands went exploring, touching her arms, cupping her breasts, then lower, to a dark secret place that sent a rocky shiver coursing through her. "It's just loving, Maxie. It's just loving."

Her eyes were huge, mesmerized. She clung to his shoulders as if they were a lifeline. He knew magic, this man. He knew how to make her moist, how to make her desperate. He knew why she ached and why she softly hit his back with her clenched fists when the aching grew too strong to endure.

"What do you want?" he gasped. "Tell me..."

"You know...I want you inside me, Connor." She was almost crying now, tears born from the intensity of their coupling. In a delirium of passion she curled her legs around him, seeking to get closer. "I need you. I want to take you in, to pull you in so deep...I need you..."

He rose up then, his hands braced on either side of her. His eyes carried a heavy-lidded sensuality as they drank in the picture she made beneath him. Never in his life had he seen such a heart-lifting, beautiful sight. "Sweet girl...you mean the world to me. This world and the next. Angel girl..."

She bit her swollen lip between her teeth as his thighs gently pushed her legs apart. She wasn't suffering so much from fear or apprehension, but because his caution was painfully frustrating. "Connor...?"

He lifted his mouth from her breast and gave her a love-hazed little smile. "What?"

"Are you deliberately taking your time?"

"Yes."

"Don't," she begged, her nails digging into the skin on his back. "I'm going *crazy*."

He kissed her mouth with infinite tenderness, then slowly began easing inside her. Despite everything Maxie had heard to the contrary, there was almost no pain. Just a blessed pleasure that promised to change to relief. She couldn't blink, couldn't take her shining eyes off his face. Her beautiful, kiss-reddened mouth parted on a soft, "Ohhhhhh..."

"You're so tight," Connor whispered, holding himself back with every ounce of willpower he possessed. "So small..."

"You're not," Maxie gasped, wanting more of him. *Want.* She felt like a child opening a birthday present. Eager, excited, curious.

She discovered that it just kept getting better. He buried himself inside her, making her gasp. Tightness, then a slow unclenching of her muscles. "Can you get deeper?"

"We're about there," he said breathlessly. "You're all right?"

"Yes. No. Please..." Loving the sensation of him inside her, she raised her hips. She saw the pleasure-pain this gave him and she had to smile, glorying in her new feminine power.

She had taken all of him and experienced a rush of delight she had never known before, but it wasn't over. Connor started to move slowly, retaining the most fragile hold on his control. He took her with him every inch of the way, lifting her higher and higher. His movements quickened with an agonizing need for release. Thrusting now, holding her eyes with his own as they climbed together. He heard her cry out as her world exploded with fireworks, and the sound pushed him over the edge. He groaned, clenching his jaw and tangling his fingers in her hair. The sweet rush seemed to go on forever with a dizzying force. It was a watershed for him, so complete and powerful, he felt as if he had died and come back with a new soul.

Two a.m.

"Connor? Are you asleep?"

"Sort of." A mumble. "What's wrong?"

"I had a bad dream." She kissed his shoulder, touching her tongue to his warm skin. "Make me feel better."

Four a.m.

"Maxie? Honey? Are you awake?"

"Mmmmm."

"I'm cold." He nuzzled the luscious valley between her ample breasts. "Can I come in and get warm?"

"Yes, please."

Connor opened his eyes to a room full of sunlight and arms full of Maxie. He was almost surprised to discover it hadn't been a dream after all. She lay on her side, her breathing deep and slow. Poor child. He'd exhausted her, and she had exhausted him right back. Looking at her, Connor could think of only one word to describe the picture she made with her sleep-flushed cheeks and bee-stung lips—*precious*. What a wonderful word.

He felt new, like a man who had been reborn, who finally understood the joy of existence. Unlike past encounters in his life, he was left with no sense of

silent loneliness, no feelings of curious disillusion-
ment. A delicate flame still burned beneath his skin,
reaching into the innermost places of his heart.

For the first time in his life, Connor understood
the difference between making love and loving. He
was ruled by his heart now, and life would never be
the same. Before this, before Maxie, it had all been
make-believe. There had been dreams of desire, il-
lusions of needs, but never the one true love.

"What took you so long to find me?" he whispered, thinking he should let her sleep and hoping
she would wake up. He sighed when she mumbled
something beneath her breath and went on sleeping.

There was simply no way he could stay here with
her and not make love to her. He rolled quietly out
of bed, then poked his head into her closet to find a
robe. There was a lovely pink chenille thing that
looked rather like a bedspread. He pulled it on, then
loved her one more time with his eyes before he left
the bedroom. The moment he was in the hall, he
could hear Boo snoring. The Calhoon family was
sleeping in.

He had planned to fix breakfast in bed for her, then
follow her about the ranch and get in her way while
she did her chores. He also had hopeful fantasies
about a hayloft. He had no idea if her barn had a
hayloft, but if it did, the possibilities were staggering.

He'd never been so happy in his life.

Boo finally roused himself as Connor walked
through the living room. The dog yawned, stretched,
yawned and stretched again. All the effort seemed to
exhaust him, but Connor nudged him toward the
front door with his bare foot. "No, you're staying

awake, boy. Go outside and do your thing, then I'll fix you a hearty breakfast. That's right. Just keep planting one paw in front of the other and you'll make it.''

Connor opened the door and stopped short. Morris, the last person in the world he had expected to see at this particular moment, was standing on the front porch with his hand raised to knock. Worse still, Morris wasn't alone. There were several vehicles parked on the road, most of them bearing the insignias of television stations. Bodies were draped over the fence, each one holding a camera focused directly on Connor. There was even a reporter sitting in the branches of a huge oak tree, clicking away. Everyone began waving and shouting questions at him, a confusing barrage of sound and movement. He heard the name *Glitter Baby* over and over. The commotion roused Boo enough to actually make him bark. Once.

''What the bloody damn *hell*…?'' Connor grabbed Morris by the shirtfront and pulled him inside, leaving Boo on the front porch to stand guard. ''Did you bring all those reporters with you?''

Morris peered at him through his wire-rimmed spectacles, mildly indignant. ''Of course I didn't bring them. I'm driving a little rental car that's not quite big enough for one.''

''I didn't mean it literally, Morris. How the hell did you find me?''

Morris blinked, looking confused. ''How did I find you? I'm a reporter, or did you forget? I went to your hotel. When you weren't there, I looked up Maxie Calhoon in the phone book. You were right, she's listed plain as day.''

''And what about everyone else?'' Connor grated

out. "It looks like the circus came to town outside. How did they find out where she was?"

"They're here because Glitter Baby is very big news. You know as well as I do after you found her it was only a matter of time before the news leaked. Hell, look on the bright side. We got the interview, thanks to my ingenious creativity. I know it's a pain in the neck to deal with all this hoopla, but the publicity will send your ratings through the roof."

"Back up, Morris." Connor's voice was low and tight. "Back up to that bit about your ingenious creativity. What did you do?"

Morris brightened, seeing an opportunity to redeem himself. "I made sure you got the interview, that's what I did! Have you had a personality transplant or something? You told me she was in financial difficulties and was arranging for a mortgage loan. I made sure it didn't go through."

"Oh, hell." Connor sank down in the couch, dropping his head into his hands. He felt sick. "I should have known something like this would happen. I should have known...."

Morris was not only baffled at this point, but more than a little peeved. "Why did you tell me about the stupid loan if you didn't want me to use it against her? You know how the game is played. It's not like you're an amateur, Connor."

"And after I told you about her loan...?" Connor's voice was barely audible. "Then what did you do?"

"I found an agency in New York who claimed she still owed them money. I gave them a little incentive to file a lien. They have no intention of letting it go to court, but by the time Maxie figures that out, we'll have the interview in the can. It worked just the way I planned. She went straight to you and agreed to do the show.'' Morris paused, waiting for a pat on the back that didn't come. ''You wanted the interview, Connor. I made sure you got it. That's what I'm supposed to do.''

It just kept getting worse. Connor dropped his head back on the sofa, hating the pain this would cause Maxie, hating his role in it. ''You're right about one thing, Morris. I'm no amateur. I should have known what would happen.''

''You're acting like this is a problem. This is what we wanted to happen.''

''Oh, yeah. It's a dream come true.'' Connor's expression was bleak. ''Where's the crew?''

''Sitting in your room at the motel. I had to bribe the desk clerk to let us in. There wasn't a spare room in town as of six o'clock this morning. The motel is overrun with reporters and camera crews. There's not a single parking space to be had on Main Street. They're swarming like locusts. I thought you might want to know before you walked into the ambush.''

As if on cue, the telephone started ringing. Connor swore beneath his breath, ran to the kitchen and flipped the ringer off. ''She's going to wake up to this zoo,'' he muttered, stomping back into the living room. ''What am I going to tell her?''

''I don't know,'' Morris said cautiously, ''but I'd change into something else if I were you. A dozen photographers just took pictures of Connor Garrett wearing a ruffled pink bathrobe. Pink's not your color, man.''

''I did this to her,'' Connor said bleakly. ''Before she met me, she managed to stay incognito. Damn it all to hell, Morris. This isn't the way I wanted things to happen.''

"Speaking of things happening…" Morris paused, choosing his words carefully. "Are you and…well, the two of you…did you…?"

"That's none of your damn business, Morris."

Morris gave a soft whistle, his eyes stretching. "I don't believe this. You did it, didn't you? You lucky dog, you did it! I worship you. Every man in America will worship you. You not only landed the interview of the decade—you actually slept with Glitter Baby!"

Before Connor could decide whether to knock him down or just throw him out, Maxie walked into the room, dressed only in Connor's white dress shirt. He had no idea what she had heard, but judging from the look on her face, she'd heard too much.

"Maxie," he said urgently, "just give me a chance—"

"Who are you?" she interrupted, staring at Morris with lifeless eyes.

Apparently Morris was struck dumb by Maxie's presence, not to mention her abbreviated attire. His mouth moved, but no sound came out. Connor threw him a look that could kill. "His name is Morris and he's part of my crew. He came out here to warn us. Look, the front yard is crawling with reporters—the entire town is crawling with reporters. I don't know how they found you, but they did."

Maxie sat down on the very edge of the sofa, her movements rigid, as if she was in terrible pain. "It doesn't matter."

"What do you mean, it doesn't matter?"

She looked up at him, meeting his eyes for the first time. Her hands were clasped in her lap. "The most important thing," she said dully, "is that you got to sleep with Glitter Baby."

# Nine

Maxie had fallen asleep in a dream and awakened in a nightmare.

It wasn't an unfamiliar nightmare; not by a long shot. She knew it by heart. The telephone had to be off the hook or it would have been ringing incessantly. The drapes were pulled. Connor had made an SOS call on his cell phone and two sheriff's deputies had appeared fifteen minutes later, sirens wailing and lights flashing. They took up their posts at the entrance to her driveway, keeping ambitious photographers and reporters out of the trees and off the fences. Unfortunately, there was no way to keep them off the main road, no legal way to take away their cameras or telephoto lenses. Maxie felt like she was trapped in the Alamo, and the enemy had somehow found his way inside with her.

"You've got to talk to me." Connor's voice was

rippling with strain through the bedroom door. "Maxie...damn it all, you know how I feel about you. *You,* not some invention of the media. I can't help it if Morris is an idiot. His mouth ran away with him, and I'm sorry. You weren't supposed to hear that."

"No, I guess not." Maxie remained curled up on her bed, staring at the closed blinds over the window and trying to think things through. It had been forty-five minutes since she had walked back in the bedroom and locked the door behind her. She had opened it just once, to toss Connor's clothes out into the hall. She knew he wouldn't leave wearing a pink bathrobe. And she wanted him to leave. "Go away, Connor."

Connor groaned and thumped his head against the door. "Maxie, I'll cancel the interview. Hell, I'll fire Morris and quit my job if you want. I'll do anything. Just...come out and talk to me. Tell me how to help you."

"I don't need your help." The room started to swim with her tears. Maxie concentrated fiercely, willing them away. She couldn't afford to fall apart. She would be *damned* if she would fall apart. She'd gone down that road once, and it hadn't been pretty. "I'm an old pro at dealing with situations like this. Being used, being lied to, being hunted down. I can handle it all."

Connor muttered an amazing string of four-letter words beneath his breath. He knew it was his fault her whereabouts had become common knowledge, albeit indirectly. Someone had tapped in on a phone conversation or bribed one of his camera crew or talked to one of the execs at the network. As Morris had pointed out, he wasn't a novice, he should have taken more precautions. If he hadn't been so damned lost in love, he *would* have been more careful.

He'd never told her, either. He'd never said he loved her, and now it was too late. She wouldn't believe him.

He sank down on the floor, resting his back against the bedroom door. He'd lost the pink bathrobe and was now wearing a wrinkled tuxedo that looked almost as stupid. How had it all come apart so quickly? Now Maxie was thrown to the wolves once again. He hurt from the knowledge that he was responsible for turning her quiet sanctuary into a prison. Whatever trust she had put in him was destroyed.

"Maxie?" There was a heavy undercurrent in his voice, an audible guilt trip of massive proportions. "Listen to me, please. You don't have to say anything, just listen. I should have protected you. I should have guarded you and kept you safe from those vultures outside. Instead…hell, I'm one of 'em. You had it all together before you met me. The cows, Harvey, your garden, this place. You built this amazing life for yourself. Then I come along and screw it all up. In the space of a few days I ruin everything you've worked so hard to build. I don't know how it happened, I never meant it to happen, but you have to believe me when I say I never wanted—"

The bedroom door opened suddenly, sending Connor backwards. He blinked upwards at Maxie from his new position on the floor. She was wearing her overalls and her hair was stuffed into a baseball cap. Other than looking pale, she seemed quite composed. Almost too composed.

"What do you think you're doing?" Connor asked.

Maxie stepped over his prone body as if he were a bug. "Have you seen my mud boots?"

"The cow-milking boots?"

"Yes."

"By the front door." Connor scrambled to his feet, trailing her into the living room. "Maxie? Where do you think you're going?"

"I have chores to do. You've been found out, Connor. There's no sense sticking around now."

Connor watched with disbelief as she pulled on her giant yellow mud boots. "You're going outside?"

"Go away, Connor. Go far, far away."

"Look, you can tell me to go away till the moon turns blue but I'm not leaving you! I know what I'm responsible for here! I have to salvage something out of this mess. I'm not leaving you to face all this craziness alone. You need me, and I'm going to be here for you. That's final."

"Are you *serious?*" Maxie gave a short, hard laugh, turning to face him. "Is that what you think? Oh, Connor, you flatter yourself. I don't need you to salvage anything. I haven't lost a damn thing, not really. Well, I suppose I did lose my virginity, but that was my choice. And please don't feel guilty for that as well, because I enjoyed myself thoroughly."

Connor closed his eyes briefly. "Maxie, you know there was more to it than that. I realize you're hurt, but don't twist this into something sordid. *Don't.*"

"I never said it was sordid. A good time was had by all. Maybe you'll get a raise for being the one to find me. That bank-loan maneuver was terribly impressive.''

''I told you, Morris did that on his own.''

''And who told Morris about the loan in the first place?''

''I did.''

Maxie shrugged. ''Like I said, you'll probably get a raise. Have you seen my gloves?''

''On the porch,'' Connor grated out. ''What are you going to do now? Walk outside dressed like that in front of fifty photographers?''

This seemed to check her. She stared long and hard at Connor, as if she couldn't quite believe what she was hearing. ''First of all,'' she said softly, ''I am dressed like this because my cows need to be milked before they explode. I would probably look better for the cameras if I changed back into that dress you bought me, but it would be hell trying to work in it and the yellow mud boots would clash. Second, I feel obligated to tell you that it isn't in your power, or anyone else's, to take away the things I hold dear in my life. I'm going outside to do what I always do. I truly don't care if my overalls aren't up to Glitter Baby's standards…or yours.''

''I don't give a damn about Glitter Baby!'' Connor tried to take her in his arms, but she backed away, shaking her head mutely. ''All right,'' he said tiredly. ''You feel you have a point to make for the reporters outside, I'll make it with you. You're not doing this alone.''

''*Hold it.*'' Maxie drew a shaky breath, her throat growing tight and painful. She wanted no misunderstandings. Now more than ever, she wanted him to understand who she really was. ''I don't want you here and I don't need you here. I'm not afraid of walking to my barn in my overalls, Connor. I'm not afraid for the world to see me as I am now. You might not believe this, but I'm *proud* of who I am. I can look into the mirror and like what I see. Can you say the same thing?'' Then, when Connor didn't answer, ''I didn't think so.''

''And what about us?''

''What about us?'' Maxie echoed tonelessly. ''There is no us, Connor. I don't know who you slept with last night, but it wasn't plain, old Maxie. So obviously, there is no us.''

''Don't do this, Maxie. You know damn well who I was with last night.''

''Actually, I don't. And that…that just isn't good enough for me. I don't make compromises any longer. It's never worth the price you pay. So if being true to myself means I might have to be alone, then I'll be alone. *And I'll be all right.*''

There were tears in her eyes, but she decided not to fight them. She figured they were as much a part of this moment as the words she spoke. Losing him hurt, but not nearly as much as losing herself would hurt.

''Don't push me away, Maxie. Let me help.''

''Help with what?'' Maxie walked over to the window, pulling the drapes wide. ''You think I need help dealing with this?'' She gestured outside, at all the little stick figures on the main road scrambling for a picture. ''No, Connor. This is child's play for me. I admit I had a bad moment there, but I'm fine now. My head is still on straight, my heart is bruised but not broken. I don't need you or anyone else to get through this. When I come back inside, I'd like you to be gone. And Connor?''

''What?''

Her eyes were misted with unshed tears, but her gaze was direct and cold. "Don't ever come back.''

Connor watched her walk out the front door, and listened as the barrage of questions came at her from all sides. Hell, it sounded as though a couple of the reporters had megaphones. Moving slowly, he went to the window, watching her walk down the front steps into the sun and give the reporters a quick wave. Then, without once glancing back at the house, she continued across the yard to the barn. She looked absurdly small and defenseless in her baggy overalls and knee-high rubber boots. She was everything he hoped for in this life and the next. His worry for her was at fever pitch, a stabbing emotion that tormented him.

He closed his eyes, taking a deep breath that didn't seem to reach his lungs. He was hurting so much, every cell in his body aching, he couldn't think. Neither could he escape the haunting voice echoing in the darkest corners of his mind: *Don't ever come back.*

He felt like he'd been turned away at the gates of heaven.

When Maxie returned from milking, the reporters were still hovering and Connor's car was gone. She'd expected it, but she didn't anticipate the emptiness that echoed through the house. Connor's absence made as deep an impact as his presence had. There were signs of their time together everywhere—the tumbled sheets on the bed, the wilted wrist corsage on the dresser, two ticket stubs for the Oakley High School homecoming dance. Here and there she could detect a whiff of his cologne, evoking powerful and sensual memories.

*You actually slept with Glitter Baby.*

She allowed herself a good hard cry at that point. Despite the show of bravado she had put on for the assembled reporters, she was hurting as she had never hurt before. It was more than her loss of privacy that devastated her. It was the knowledge that she would never be free of Glitter Baby. Whatever her feelings were for Connor—and she very much feared she loved him—she was justifiably frightened of his motives. He had set out to find the phenomenon known as Glitter Baby, and that was precisely what he had done. She had deluded herself into thinking he was attracted to Maxie Calhoon, but she knew now how horribly wrong she had been. Judging from Morris's comments, sleeping with Glitter Baby was a feather in Connor's cap.

She called her mother and filled her in on everything that had happened. Well, almost everything.

"What do you mean, 'When we got up the press was everywhere'?" Natalie demanded. "What exactly does *we* mean?"

I'd make a terrible spy, Maxie thought. I have a big mouth. "I meant me," she explained hastily. "I meant when *I* got up this morning."

"You're lying. I've always been able to tell when you were lying, Maxie. Something happened last night, didn't it? After Connor took you to the dance—"

"Mother, this isn't about my love life. Will you please just listen—"

"Hold it," Natalie interrupted. "This is very interesting to me. I wasn't aware you *had* a love life."

I did, Maxie thought. Almost. "What I had or didn't have isn't the point. The secret is out, my house is besieged and Connor Garrett is no different than anyone else. He wanted to use Glitter Baby as his own personal stepping stone. And," she added with a watery sniff, "I let him."

"Well, so much for feminine intuition," Natalie sighed. "I hate to tell you this, but I kind of thought you and he might…well, you know. I guess I was wrong."

"I know the feeling," Maxie said. She slashed at her tears with an impatient hand. It made her furious when she gave into self-pity like this. She reminded herself she wasn't a victim any longer. In the great scheme of things, this was just a little bump in a long road. "I don't know what I'm going to do. I'm back to where I started a few days ago. No money. No mortgage loan. And no Con—" she caught herself at the last minute. "And no options."

"Well," Natalie said realistically, "be happy you aren't in town. This place is positively infested with camera-carrying buttheads. And that's exactly what I called them when they had the gall to pound on my door at the crack of dawn this morning."

Despite her woes, Maxie giggled. "Good for you."

"In fact, I think I'll pack a bag and come and stay with you for a couple of days. If we're going to be recluses for a while, we may as well be recluses together. I'll stop and pick up some groceries on my way."

"I'll let the guards know you're coming," Maxie

replied. "Don't forget the SpaghettiOs. I'm out. And some chocolate. And some—"

"I get the picture. The cavalry is coming, sweetheart."

Maxie hung up the phone, then walked back to her bedroom and curled up on the bed in a nice fetal position. It was supposed to be therapeutic, but she still felt caged. She felt oppressively exhausted, worn to her very soul. Hopelessness and helplessness washed over her like a crushing tide, stealing the breath from her body.

She missed him.

The first photographs in the scandal rags appeared the very next morning. Connor wanted to punch somebody when he saw them. Maxie was pictured in her boots and overalls, with various headlines. Glitter Baby Surfaces—As Old McDonald. Glitter Baby at the Fat Farm. And the most hurtful of all: Glitter Baby Tragedy. Details of a Nervous Breakdown.

And, of course, photographs of Connor wearing a frilly robe were right there alongside Maxie's. According to the cutlines below the pictures, Connor was a "former football star turned reporter and crossdresser." Morris had been right. Pink really wasn't his color. He supposed he might have found it funny under different circumstances. But nothing was funny about the terrible mess he'd created.

He was still at the Oakley Motel, crammed into a room with two double beds, members of the camera crew and Morris. He'd stopped trying to contact Maxie. Her phone had been off the hook since the day before. He didn't really blame her for being angry, but he refused to give up before he had a chance to tell her his side of the story. His crew was getting antsy. When they asked him if they could go home, they got a flat no. When Morris started talking about Alan Greenspan again, he nearly got a lot more than a flat no. It was all Connor could do to keep his fist out of Morris's face. In his calmer moments, he knew Morris had done nothing out of the ordinary. Sleight-of-hand tricks came along with the profession. They'd never bothered Connor before, but now he felt no better than the tabloid reporters gathered in the lobby downstairs. Just another member of the rat pack.

Around noon there was a knock at the door. Since there was a policeman stationed outside to turn away nosy reporters, Connor immediately thought it might be Maxie. He made it to the door at light speed.

But it wasn't Maxie. Connor didn't even try to hide the disappointment on his face when he saw Jacob Stephens.

"It's you," he said flatly.

Jacob lifted one gray eyebrow. He was a short man with a barrel chest and a soft-spoken demeanor that disguised a razor-sharp intellect. "It is," he confirmed. "And judging from your reaction, you were hoping for someone else."

Connor forced a tight smile as he ushered his godfather into the room. "Well, I've learned we don't always get what we want."

Jacob looked around the room, counting heads. "There are too many people in this room. Could you boys excuse us, please?"

Jacob was a mild-mannered man, but a shrewd and demanding boss who never gave orders twice. The room cleared in a heartbeat. Connor sat down on the edge of the bed, motioning for Jacob to take the only chair in the room. "Sorry the accommodations are so tight. There's not a room to be found in this town."

"So you said when you called me last night." Jacob sat down gingerly, smoothing the creases in his slacks. "Discovering Glitter Baby in Oakley was like discovering gold. Everyone wants their chance to try their luck."

"Don't call her Glitter Baby," Connor said quietly. "She has a name—Maxie Calhoon."

Jacob observed his star reporter with keen eyes. The changes in Connor in just a few days were remarkable. His carefree attitude had been replaced by exhaustion and strain. He hadn't shaved, and his light blue shirt was wrinkled, as if he'd slept in it. "You don't look well," he offered mildly.

"I'm fine."

"You have two different-colored socks on."

Connor looked down at his feet. "So I do. Maybe I'll start a new fad...one brown argyle, one white athletic sock."

Jacob couldn't quite discipline his smile. "Or pink bathrobes with ruffles. Very fetching, I must say."

Connor rolled his eyes. "My old football buddies are going to get a kick out of that. I'll never live it down. Jacob, I'm sorry I messed this thing up. I know you needed this interview."

"We still have the interview," Jacob replied.

Connor stared at him. He had to open his mouth two or three times before any sound came out. "What do you mean? Yesterday she tossed me out of her house."

"All right, I'll rephrase it. *I* have the interview.

Maxie Calhoon got in touch with me late last night. She's willing to go ahead with the interview as long as you're not the one posing the questions.''

"I see." It took Connor a moment to recover from that one. "I suppose I can't blame her. Are you planning on doing it yourself?''

"That was what she suggested," Jacob replied. "Rather firmly. She said she needed the money, but that wasn't her whole motivation. Apparently there are a few things she would like to set straight.''

"I guess that's that, then." Connor's jaw was clenched hard enough to crack a filling. "The lady knows what she wants.''

"Unlike most women." Jacob's brows drew together thoughtfully. He'd known Connor Garrett all his life, but this somber-faced man bore no resemblance to the brash, carefree spirit he was familiar with. He couldn't remember the last time he'd seen Connor in a blue funk. "Remember what I told you about never letting pleasure interfere with business?''

Connor colored hotly. "Yes.''

"Did you let pleasure interfere with business?''

Connor considered this thoughtfully. "*Pleasure* is too mild a word, I'm afraid. I let love interfere with business.''

Jacob gave a soft whistle, his eyes stretching. "Well, this *is* a surprise, I must say. I'd just about given up on you finding someone special. You never seemed to want it badly enough.''

"I can promise you," Connor muttered softly, "I want Maxie Calhoon more than I've ever wanted anything in my life. Unfortunately, she doesn't feel the same way about me.''

Jacob stood up, wandering to the window. With his back turned to Connor, he said, "Are you sure?"

"She made it pretty damn clear," Connor confirmed bleakly.

Jacob turned to look at Connor, an inscrutable expression on his face. "I had a little talk with Morris. I know pretty much everything. What happened wasn't your fault."

Connor felt like he was coming apart inside his skin. He stood up and started pacing, his hands shoved deep into his pockets. "That's where you're wrong. I know how this business works, Jacob. I knew what would happen, but I didn't want to face it. I was taking every opportunity to spend more time with her, regardless of the risks. Now she's the one paying for it."

Jacob shook his head in bemusement. "Amazing. I've never seen you exhibit such remorse, particularly for something you didn't do. It's quite extraordinary."

"Was I so bad?"

"Oh no, quite the contrary. You were *always* in good spirits. That's why I worried about you. All your life, everything came so easily to you. I'm not sure you learned how to value anything. You never cared for anyone enough to stick your neck out and risk getting hurt. And without that vulnerability, love can't exist."

"Well, I sure as hell care now," Connor muttered. "My neck is stuck out all the way to China, and I'm hurting like there's no tomorrow. For all the good it's doing me."

"Would you rather we didn't go ahead with the story?"

Connor scowled. He was still smarting from the knowledge Maxie wanted Jacob to conduct the interview. "It has nothing to do with me anymore. You make the call."

"What do you mean, it has nothing to do with you? You've been on this story from the beginning."

"I'm quitting," Connor said abruptly. "I'm going to take care of the lien on Maxie's house, then I'm going home. I have no idea what I'm going to do, but it's not going to be in front of a camera. I'm sorry if this puts you in a bad position, Jacob. You've always believed in me, and I appreciate it more than I can say. I'd do anything for you, but I just can't go on like nothing's happened."

Jacob put his hand on Connor's shoulder, squeezing gently. "I'm not worried about doing the interview, son. I was a reporter for twenty years, so I figure I can handle myself."

"Good," Connor said in a hollow voice. "Everything's settled then."

"I'd like you to do me one favor, however. Stick around until we have the interview wrapped. You're the expert, and I'd like you around for backup. I'm bound to be a bit rusty. I'm sure I'm going to need all the help I can get. After that, I'll accept your resignation and wish you the best."

Connor smiled faintly, not at all fooled by Jacob's humble demeanor. "You won't need me, Jacob. You're a professional."

"Humor me."

Connor shrugged, rubbing the back of his neck tiredly. "Fine. Whatever. After all you've done for me, I suppose that's the least I can do. But I warn you, Maxie is not going to like it. The last thing she said to me was—and I quote—*don't ever come back.*''

"Really?" Jacob looked amused. "Another first. As a rule, women seem to be quite…cooperative…where you're concerned. Confidentially, I always thought if I'd been born looking more like you—a little more hair, a few more inches—I wouldn't have ended up as a lonely bachelor at fifty-three. This girl of yours must be something quite special."

"This girl of mine…" Connor said softly, a flicker of pain contorting his face. He closed his eyes, seeing her image burning brightly on his retinas. "I don't know how to stop caring. I don't want to stop caring. She's one of a kind, Jacob."

"I've never met her, but after listening to you, I'm inclined to agree." Jacob's brown-eyed gaze was infinitely kind. "Don't despair, dear boy. We never know what fate has in store for us. Why, that's half the joy of living, waiting to see what happens next."

"Half the joy," Connor muttered, "or half the pain?"

"Gracious, she's turned you into a cynic in a few short days. I must meet her immediately. Take a shower, round up the crew and meet me downstairs in one hour. She's expecting me at noon."

"Expecting *you,*" Connor said darkly. "*I'm* going to be a surprise."

"Indeed you are." Smiling, Jacob headed for the door. "This should be highly entertaining."

# Ten

**M**axie knew there had been some horrible cosmic error in her life, a tragedy of major proportions. Not only was she walking around with a wounded heart, but—horror of horrors—she'd lost her appetite, as well.

"Force yourself," Natalie said sternly, facing her daughter across the kitchen table. "I made you chicken noodle soup, which cures everything. But it isn't going to help a darn bit unless you eat it."

"It's not going to cure what ails me," Maxie mumbled, stirring circles in the soup with her spoon. "I'm permanently damaged."

Natalie sighed heavily, knowing her daughter's predilection for high drama. "Dear hart, you're much stronger than you think. If you don't want your soup, eat some chocolate. Chocolate always makes you feel better."

"I know," Maxie replied in a soggy voice. "It's really making me mad. That damn man has ruined *chocolate* for me."

"He's an absolute monster, dear. If he were here right now, I would deck him."

Maxie blinked. "Deck him? Mother—"

"To mislead you like that, to trick you into letting your guard down, to take advantage of your friendship. Well, there are no words for men like him. And to think, he seems so personable and trustworthy, like a Boy Scout. Aren't you grateful he's out of the picture once and for all?"

"Ecstatic."

"If I were you," Natalie continued, warming to her subject, "I would sue the man. I would press charges. I would—"

"Mother, you're getting worked up." For some obscure reason, Maxie felt obliged to set the record straight. "It's not like he kidnapped me. He just...tricked me. Sort of."

"Like I said, a monster. Any man who would lie like a rug just to get close to a woman because she was famous—"

"I never said he actually lied. He just didn't tell me the truth."

"The truth about what, dear?" Natalie stared at her daughter expectantly.

"Well..." Maxie's mind went blank. Feeling more frustrated by the minute, she stood up and carried her dishes to the sink. "Never mind. I know what he did and he knows what he did. I don't want to talk about this anymore. I'm going to change my clothes. Jacob Stephens should be here with the television crew any minute."

"What are you going to wear?"

Maxie shrugged, not really caring one way or the other. "Jeans, I suppose. I'm not Glitter Baby anymore. I don't need to worry about making an impression."

"You *might*," Natalie suggested helpfully, "want to do your hair up in a little French twist or—"

"I'm not going to worry about my hair." Maxie wasn't trying to be difficult. She simply couldn't summon any interest in her appearance. When it came right down to it, she couldn't summon much interest in anything. "I'm sorry, really. I know I'm not much fun right now. I just want this interview done with."

"You're quite amazing, honey," Natalie said softly. "You have remarkable courage."

"I'm not amazing at all. It's like you said. I've become ordinary. I just need to let the rest of the world in on that fact and maybe they'll leave me alone." Her eyes misted over with tears, her shoulders bowed like a tired child's. "I don't know what's happening in me. I'm a mess. I'm afraid it's going to hurt like this forever. I thought I'd paid my dues, figured I had put Glitter Baby behind me once and for all. And then, then when I finally find someone…"

She cried then, and not for the first time that day. Natalie held her daughter in her arms just as she had the first day Maxie had returned to Wyoming to begin healing. "You're far stronger than you think, Maxie," she whispered. "The rest of your life begins today. Trust me when I tell you everything is going to be all right."

"I was so sure," Maxie choked out. "I thought

he looked at me and saw *me*. And now...now all I feel is this terrible emptiness."

Natalie stroked her daughter's hair, waiting until the shudders that coursed through her body subsided. "Unfortunately, you're going to look a little puffy around the eyes if you don't stop crying. What with the interview and everything," Natalie glanced over Maxie's shoulder at the kitchen window and froze. "Uh-oh. Oh, dear. This is bad."

"What? What's wrong?" Still rubbing her eyes, Maxie turned and glanced out the window. Her eyes widened and her pity-fest immediately turned into a dry, flat panic. Two television vans were parked in her driveway...right behind a yellow compact rental car. A distinguished-looking, balding fellow in a tweed jacket was striding towards the house, right beside a very tall man with rainbow-brown hair and a tense expression on his face.

"I told him *never* to come back," Maxie said fiercely. "I said *never*."

"It appears he didn't listen." Natalie sighed and looked her daughter up and down. "You're a little splotchy, honey. You might want to do some salvage work before you face him. Then again, this would certainly be a good opportunity to show him you truly don't care a lick how you—"

"Keep them busy," Maxie told her, already halfway to the bedroom. "Tell them I just came in from milking. Buy me some time."

"I thought you didn't care how you looked?" Natalie called after her daughter.

"I don't. I don't give a damn."

Natalie heard the bedroom door slam shut. At almost the same instant, the doorbell rang. "This should be interesting,'' she murmured, a tiny smile playing with the corner of her lips as she went to answer the door. ''Who said life in the country was dull?''

Connor was a bundle of raw nerves. He wanted to see Maxie in the worst way, but not like this. Not with his boss and her mother looking on. Not with a television crew waiting outside and Maxie apparently locked in her bedroom again. This was not a good situation, and he very much regretted letting Jacob talk him into coming.

''Do you think your daughter will be long?'' Jacob inquired of Natalie. ''I'd like to do the outside shots while we have good light.''

''She just came in from milking,'' Natalie lied obediently. ''She's cleaning up a bit. You know, Mr. Stephens, you're not at all what I expected.''

''Really?'' Jacob smiled politely. ''What *did* you expect?''

Natalie waved her hand in the air. ''Oh, you know, someone a bit more…imposing. After all, you're the head of a big television network. I expected someone rather blustery and bossy, to be frank.''

''Perhaps someone taller?'' Jacob suggested.

Natalie smiled prettily. ''I would never say that.''

''I suppose it must be rather hard on you,'' Jacob went on innocently. ''Being so unnaturally tall yourself, you probably have to look down on everyone.''

''Not everyone. Just the short people.''

Connor's panic was increasing by the second. If this barbed conversation continued, he feared Jacob and Natalie would come to blows. ''You know,'' he said quickly, "You two have something in common. Jacob collects antiques with a passion."

"Are you interested in antiques, Mrs. Calhoon?" Jacob inquired. "Perhaps a little hobby of yours?"

"Something like that," Natalie replied with sugary sweetness. "I have a little *hobby shop* in town."

Connor planted a smile on his face and stepped between them. "Natalie, maybe you should see what's keeping your daughter."

"My daughter will come out when she's good and ready to come out. I don't mind telling you, Connor, she wasn't too happy to see you arrive with Mr. Stephens. She was under the impression you weren't going to be involved in the interview."

"He's here at my request," Jacob said smoothly. "It's been a while since I sat in front of the camera, and there's no one better than Connor to guide me through it."

Just then Maxie came sailing into the room in a cloud of perfume. "How lovely to meet you, Mr. Stephens," she said graciously, holding out her hand. "I'm Maxie Calhoon."

Ordinarily, Jacob was the most sophisticated of men, but Maxie's staggering beauty rendered even him momentarily speechless. She had changed into white linen slacks paired with a body-hugging white sweater. Her hair was loose, framing her face in a soft, dark cloud. She had applied her makeup with an expert hand, emphasizing her glorious eyes and the lavish curves of her generous lips. "Well," he managed finally, "at last I know what all the hoopla is about. No wonder you're having trouble shaking the media, Maxie. With the exception of your dear mother," and he gave Natalie an overly sweet smile of his own, "who I've just met, you're quite the most beautiful woman I have ever seen."

Maxie shook her head modestly. "It's all done with mirrors, Mr. Stephens."

"Call me Jacob," he replied easily. "I'm certain we're going to get along famously. For a good interview, one must be comfortable, and I'll do everything in my power to make certain you are."

Connor was tired of being invisible. "You look beautiful," he told Maxie bluntly. "But I think I prefer the overalls. You're a bit more approachable in overalls."

"Since you won't be approaching me," Maxie said without looking at him, "we won't have a problem. Shall we start filming, Jacob? I thought I would give you a tour of the place while we chat. Later on we can set up in here for a more formal discussion. And please feel free to ask me anything. I have nothing to hide."

Connor was stinging from her rebuff, but his overriding concern was Maxie's protection. "That's not a good idea, Maxie," he said. "Go over a list of questions and approve them or throw them out. You need to know what's coming."

Maxie turned to face him for the first time. "That's so true," she said coolly. "If I had known what was coming when you walked into my life, I could have saved myself a great deal of time and trouble. What *are* you doing here, Connor?"

"I brought him," Jacob intervened quickly, putting a casual arm around Maxie's shoulders and turning her toward the front door. "I thought he might be useful. Don't worry about Connor, Maxie. The only thing you need to be concerned with is looking wonderful for the camera, and you've already managed that. Shall we begin?''

Jacob and Maxie left, neither of them giving Connor a second look. He walked mutely to the window, watching Jacob introduce Maxie to the crew. Without exception, the men wore identical expressions of stunned admiration.

''She knocks men down with a simple smile,'' he commented tonelessly to Natalie. ''They fall like dominoes. What's amazing to me is that they don't see the real beauty, they don't know what's inside her heart. She's a miracle.''

''From what she told me,'' Natalie countered, ''you weren't much interested in the real Maxie Calhoon. It was all about Glitter Baby.''

''It was *never* about Glitter Baby,'' Connor replied fiercely, facing Natalie with burning eyes. ''Never, not since the first day I met her. She showed me her mind and her heart and her soul, and I fell in love for the first time in my life. But she doesn't believe that, and she never will.''

Natalie considered this for a moment, her brows drawn together thoughtfully. ''My daughter spent eight years wearing a mask, Connor. Everyone she met was drawn to Glitter Baby, no one was interested in Maxie Calhoon. She was hurt terribly. She had no identity, no self-esteem. Never once in all that time did she date anyone seriously. Never once.''

''I know,'' Connor whispered softly, a shadow clouding his eyes. ''She was so afraid they didn't want *her*. And now...now she believes I didn't want her, either. She's so damned vulnerable.''

Something in Natalie's features relaxed. She placed a gentle hand on Connor's shoulder, her Mona

Lisa smile an exact replica of her daughter's. "You understand, then. That's good. Maxie's endured enough pain for one lifetime. All she wants now is to have her own safe place in the universe. And I think it would be absolutely lovely," she paused, choosing her words with care, "if she had someone to share that place with her. She's been alone so long."

"How do I convince her? How do I make her believe I don't give a damn about Glitter Baby? I hate hearing that name, I hate looking into her eyes and seeing the wounds when she thinks about that time in her life." His bleak gaze strayed back to the window. Maxie, Jacob and the camera crew were heading towards the barn. He wanted to go outside and pick her up in his arms, carry her away from any reminders of Glitter Baby. He felt like he was losing her all over again with every step she took. "Believe me, Natalie. I want nothing from your daughter but her love."

"I do believe you," Natalie said quietly. "Now you need to convince her. It's not going to be easy, either. She has a bit of her mother's feisty spirit."

Connor had to smile at that. "She does. You know, you were giving Jacob a pretty good run for his money a few minutes ago."

Natalie laughed. "I was bad, wasn't I? Come along, then. Let's go outside and I'll make nice."

"Maxie doesn't want me around."

"And your point is…?"

Connor was broken-hearted, frustrated and depressed, but he found himself laughing with helpless abandon. "Natalie, you're a remarkable woman. I can see why Maxie is so special."

"Thank you." Natalie looked at him with gentle reassurance. "I like you, Connor. More importantly, I believe my daughter loves you, whether she admits it or not. I was testing her before you arrived today. Try as I might, she wouldn't let me say anything truly bad about you."

"I guess that's something," Connor muttered doubtfully. "Maybe if I just let Jacob do his thing and stay in the background, she won't pitch a fit."

"Stranger things have happened," Natalie replied breezily. "But I wouldn't count on it. Come along, then. Once more into the breach, my friend."

It turned out to be a very bad idea.

Things went well for the first few minutes. Other than giving Connor a hostile look when he and Natalie walked up, Maxie completely ignored him. She was leaning against the fence, with thirty cows in the background acting as local scenery. The camera crew was ready, the equipment in place. Jacob adjusted his tie, gave Maxie's shoulder a reassuring squeeze and the filming began.

"To say this interview is rather special," he began, smiling at the camera, "is a vast understatement. I'm standing in this beautiful country setting with Glitter Baby, the woman who disappeared—"

"*Cut,*" Connor yelled.

"Cut?" Jacob threw Connor a quelling look. "You are not here as a director," he said. "Did you ever hear me ask you to be the director?"

Connor flushed, but persevered stubbornly. "Jacob, you're talking as if Maxie *is* Glitter Baby. You can't do that, you can't feed the media that kind of bait. They'll never leave her alone."

Jacob glowered. "Fine, you had your input. Now if you'll allow me to continue?" He signalled the cameraman and started again. "I'm standing in this beautiful country setting just a few miles north of Oakley, Wyoming—"

"*Cut!*" Connor pushed his way past the cameras, stepping between Maxie and Jacob. "Why don't you just draw a freaking map for the world? Hell, give her address and phone number while you're at it! Jacob, you've got to protect her anonymity. You can't just stand there and blurt out—"

"Have you lost your mind?" Jacob demanded, suddenly looking much taller than five feet six inches. "Do I have to put masking tape over your mouth, or are you going to let me do this interview?"

"Then *do* the damn interview, but use a little professionalism. Is that so hard? Hell, you've been in this business for thirty years. You know the ropes. Why are you acting like an amateur?"

Maxie stared at Connor, her mouth half-open. The members of the camera crew looked at one another with mute ecstasy. Natalie covered a laugh by clearing her throat.

"Are you quite through?" Jacob asked softly, his eyes promising retribution. "Any further instructions?"

"No," Connor said, aware that he was acting like an idiot, but quite unable to monitor his mouth. Love was hell, he discovered, on one's dignity. "Just…be careful with her."

"I will try my poor best," Jacob grated out with an overdose of sincerity. "May I proceed, please?"

Connor disappeared behind the cameras, retreating to the shade of a pine tree with Natalie. He felt helpless, barely stifling a desire to smash every camera in the vicinity.

"Well," Natalie said, when she was quite sure she had her giggles under control. "That was...quite extraordinary. Do you take such a fierce personal interest in all your interviews?"

"No," Connor said flatly, hotly flushed from the neck up.

"That may be a blessing. Your career might have been rather short."

Connor shrugged. They were too far away from Jacob and Maxie to hear what was being said, but that didn't stop Connor from trying to read their lips. "It doesn't matter, anyway. Before we drove out here today, I quit."

Natalie regarded him with disbelieving eyes. "You what?"

"I quit. Hell, why do think Jacob didn't fire me just now? I beat him to it. I don't have the stomach for this business any longer. I don't know if I've suddenly gone insane or if I'm just crazy in love. It doesn't really matter *why,* anyway. I did what I had to do."

"I wonder what Maxie will say about that," Natalie murmured.

"I doubt she'll care." Connor rubbed the back of his neck, suddenly feeling drained. "Look, I'm sorry, but I can't put myself through this, Natalie. I'm making everything more difficult than it is. I have to get out of here. I'm going home."

"Just give it a little more time," Natalie pleaded. "Don't do anything final. Give her a chance to think about things."

"She knows what she's doing. Your daughter isn't

a victim any longer. She's in charge of her life, and that's what she's always wanted. Tell her...just tell her..."

"Tell her what?" Natalie asked softly, staring at him intently.

"I don't know." Connor's eyes focused one last time on the lovely, dark-haired woman haloed in golden sunlight. She was animated, talking easily with Jacob, using her hands to express her thoughts. She was the most beautiful and vibrant creature on God's green earth. He had to force himself to release her from his sight.

"Tell her I'm proud of her," he said.

# Eleven

"**I**'m sorry," the ticket agent told Connor. "There's going to be a slight delay boarding the commuter flight. There's a moose on the runway."

Connor was in a foul mood. He'd driven four hours from Oakley to Jackson Hole, arriving at midnight only to find the next flight was not until 8:00 a.m. the following morning. He'd found himself a bar and passed a couple of hours downing shots of tequila. Well-oiled and wobbly, he'd taken a cab back to the terminal and curled up for the rest of the night on a chair obviously made of the hardest hardwood in the world. When he roused himself several hours later, he was literally bruised from head to foot. He also had a raging hangover, which was being irritated by this young woman's perkiness.

"What kind of airport allows moose to run free on the runway?" he demanded, leaning heavily against the counter. His balance wasn't quite up to par. "This never happens in Los Angeles."

The ticket agent showed him dimples and a toothy smile. "You're so *funny*. We all know moose don't live in cities, don't we?"

"We know nothing," Connor muttered, "except that we have a killer headache. Where can I get some aspirin?"

She giggled, apparently finding him terribly amusing. "Someone's in a grouchy mood," she said, blond curls bouncing energetically. "You can buy aspirin at the gift shop, just down the corridor. By the time you get back, I'm sure we'll be ready to board. No errant moose will get the best of Rocky Mountain Airlines! Is there anything else I can do for you?"

"No," Connor growled. His stomach was threatening revenge for all the tequila he'd consumed. Connor had never been a good drinker, had never really enjoyed drinking. He had thought to block his growing depression, but the alcohol had only increased it. From now on, he vowed silently, he was a milk drinker.

Which made him think of cows, which made him think of Maxie, which made him even more depressed. Leaving her, knowing she was beyond his reach forever, had given new meaning to the word *despair*. The pain was with him all the time, drunk or sober. It prickled along his spine, it blurred his vision periodically, it made his heart hurt in his chest. Now that he knew what it was to be with her, how it felt to be so alive and fulfilled by her, how could he ever survive without her? The contrast was unbearable.

The first thing he noticed in the gift shop was the newspaper rack, overflowing with scandal rags. Of the six magazines offered for sale, five had cover stories on Glitter Baby and her new cross-dressing companion. Connor wondered how he would ever forget her if her picture was going to be everywhere he looked. He knew that smile personally, he knew the magic in her violet eyes, he knew how her lips felt against his. The photographs only reminded him of how much he had lost. It seemed that everywhere he turned, there was yet another picture. Why did the only love of his life have to be one of the most recognizable faces in America?

Heartsick, Connor tugged his baseball cap further down on his head, on the off-chance someone might recognize him as the star of the pink-bathrobe fiasco. He wasn't in the mood for any complications; he was too busy being miserable. He was standing in line with his bottle of aspirin when a conversation between a couple of young men behind him caught his attention.

"Man, she's the hottest thing on the planet. Whenever I'm scoring with another woman, I close my eyes and pretend it's her. So when you think about it, I've slept with Glitter Baby a hundred times."

"Who hasn't?" his companion said. "You can tell just by looking at her picture that she's a nympho. That's not something you can just put on for a camera. No, she wants it, that's for sure."

"I'd like to be the one to give it to her."

That did it. Connor turned to face them in a single fluid movement, a blood vessel throbbing wildly in his temple. Fury burned in his dark eyes and gave a white-hot edge to his voice. "I'd advise you two to keep your filthy mouths shut."

"Or what?" The taller of the two took a step forward, pushing hard on Connor's chest. "What are you, some damned missionary?"

"Yes." Connor smiled slowly. "And I'm going to help you two get to heaven...right now." Before the fellow could react, Connor swung, planting a fist directly in his face. The force with which he connected was astonishing. As a matter of fact, he was pretty sure he'd broken a couple of knuckles. Before his target hit the floor, he'd rounded on the second man. This time he missed the nose, which he was aiming for, but managed to land a pretty good facer anyway. The man shook his head a second, then with a roar lunged at Connor, knocking over the candy stand in the process. Somewhere in the middle of it all, Connor heard a woman shouting for security. He ducked a punch and swung again, sending his opponent to the floor amidst rolling packages of candy. At that point someone new entered the fight, telling him to calm down and trying to grab him from behind. Before Connor could shake him, a determined security guard put an end to the melee by bringing his nightstick down on the back of Connor's head.

At that point it was lights out.

Once it became public knowledge that Jacob Stephens had landed an exclusive interview, the flurry of reporters staking out the ranch gradually began to thin out. Maxie was tremendously relieved now she had no more secrets to hide. Jacob had been wonderful, quite protective after Connor had left the scene. He'd gently led Maxie through the dark recollections of her anorexia, giving her the opportunity and encouragement to speak her mind. She left no doubt of her opinion of society's infatuation with starved bodies and superficial beauty. What other people thought of her, Maxie stressed, was no longer her business. She only hoped that there were those who would benefit by her mistakes.

She was a professional in front of the cameras. While those who knew her well might detect the shadows in her eyes, the public at large would see a young woman with strong new convictions. Maxie held it together beautifully, bidding Jacob and the camera crew farewell later that evening. She continued to hold it together throughout dinner, talking with her mother about everything in the world but Connor Garrett. She slept on the sofa, giving Natalie the bedroom. That worked well, as there was no audience to witness the full eight hours of misery and sniffles, and not a minute of sleep she finally indulged in.

The following morning Natalie took one look at her daughter's swollen eyes and offered to miss her hair appointment that morning.

"Don't be silly. Go on ahead, I have tons of work to do." Maxie walked her mother outside, waving to the guards at the gate. "Bring back some donuts or something. We'll treat the men in blue when you come back."

Natalie stared at Maxie's pallid face. "Your smile," she said softly, "doesn't begin to reach your eyes."

After Natalie drove away, Maxie retreated into the house. It was quite true she had tons of work to do, she just didn't have the heart to do it. She curled up on the sofa and tried to lose a few of the empty hours in a much-needed nap. Exhaustion finally kicked in and she drifted off, tossing and turning fitfully. Even in sleep she couldn't escape dreams of Connor and the single night they had spent together. Her mind told her she was a fool; her body ached for his touch.

Her restless sleep was interrupted by a tentative knock at the door. The guards wouldn't have let anyone unauthorized approach the house, Maxie knew. Which meant it had to be someone from the television crew.

Irrationally, Maxie felt her spirits lift. Maybe, just maybe, the end to her love story hadn't been written yet.

It was a short trip for her spirits. They plummeted the instant they recognized the sheepish-looking fellow on the front porch.

"Morrie," she said flatly.

"Actually, it's Morris. But under the circumstances, you can call me any damn thing you want." He paused, nervously pushing his glasses up on the bridge of his nose. "Can I come in, please? We need to talk."

"Is it something about the interview?"

"No. Although that's what I told the guards." Morris shuffled from one foot to the other. "It's about...well, it's about Connor. There's been a little misunderstanding. Actually, a big misunderstanding. If you'll just let me explain, I promise I'll go away as far and as fast as I can and never inflict myself upon you again."

Maxie told herself to send him packing even as she swung the door wide. She opened the door, waving him in. "Fine. You have two minutes."

Morris walked into the living room, giving Maxie a wide berth. She looked very beautiful, but very hostile. "I'll make this quick," he said rapidly, conscious of his two-minute deadline. "I am a bad person. I didn't think so, but now I know what I did was bad, especially for you and Connor."

Maxie shook her head, completely confused. "I don't know what you mean. Do *you* know what you mean?"

"Of course I know what I mean," Morris muttered. "Look, when Connor told me initially that you'd turned him down for an interview, I did what every good assistant does. I fixed things."

"And you did that by...?"

"I'm the one responsible for derailing your mortgage loan at the bank. It was *my* brainchild, not Connor's. I thought he would be happy when your old agency slapped a lien on your place. They weren't going through with it anyway. They knew they were on shaky legal ground. And I figured the end always justifies the means, you know? Only this time it didn't."

Maxie's legs turned rubbery. She sank down on the sofa, looking up at Morris with unblinking eyes. "It didn't?"

"Connor has been a great boss, the best. Man, he taught me everything. Then, when he finds someone who really matters to him, I mess things up for him. He was furious when he found out what I did. No, it was worse than furious—he was devastated." Morris groaned, slapping his forehead with the palm of his hand. "I'm an idiot. When I saw him here with you that morning I knew what a terrible mistake I'd made. He didn't give a damn about the interview.

The only thing he could think of was you and how all of it would affect you. You knew he quit, didn't you?"

"Yes, but I thought it was because he lost the interview. I thought it was just sour grapes."

"Hell, Connor isn't capable of that. He quit because he didn't want any part of a business that had hurt you so badly. He took off for Jackson Hole last night looking like the living dead."

Maxie flinched. "He's gone?"

Morris was glad she was sitting down. She had just lost all color in her face, and he didn't know CPR. Gingerly he sat beside her, patting her hand awkwardly. "No, not really. I mean, he would have been back in L.A. today if they hadn't put him in jail."

Suddenly Maxie's numb fingers came alive, closing over Morris's hand in a death grip. "Jail? *Jail?* What are you talking about?"

Her fingernails, Morris realized painfully, were digging into his skin. "He's in the Jackson Hole jail," Morris explained, carefully removing her fingers from his hand. "He's all right, just incarcerated. He called me before I came here. Apparently a couple of guys in the airport saw a newspaper and made a comment about you Connor didn't like. He knocked them both cold before a security guard knocked him out. I told him he shouldn't act like that in airports. He told me to go to hell, but first drive down and bail him out." He paused, allowing this to sink in. "I'm on my way there now," he added. "I just wanted you to know everything before I left."

Maxie let out her breath in a long, shaky sigh. "Ohh, what a bloody idiot," she whispered.

"I know," Morris said humbly. "I am an idiot, but I wanted—"

"Not you," Maxie replied. "Me."

Morris brightened. "Yes, indeed! You were very wrong. You might think about having a nice talk with him once I get him sprung. Now that he finally found you it would be a terrible shame if he lost you. And vice versa."

Maxie wasn't listening to Morris any longer. She was finally listening to her own somewhat inexperienced heart. She'd spent so many years living on the edge, building walls between herself and the rest of the world, all to keep from being hurt. But now she was healed, and she needn't hide from the real world. She was finally strong enough and wise enough to know that love was well worth the risk.

Connor was worth the risk.

Maxie still didn't know the end of her love story—there was just no predicting that. But if ever there was a man worth putting one's trust in, worth sharing hopes and dreams for the future with, it was the beautiful, decent, selfless, golden-eyed Adonis languishing in the Jackson Hole jail.

"He fought for my honor," she said, violet eyes growing misty.

"That he did," Morris acknowledged, a little smile teasing his mouth. "And landed in jail for his efforts. What a shame. Still, if you'd like me to bring him back here after I rescue him—"

"That won't be necessary." The smile of sweet anticipation that spread from her lips to her amazing eyes caused poor Morris's heart to falter. "I'll rescue him."

Morris looked doubtful. "I'm not sure the Jackson Hole jail is the best place for a reunion."

"He rescued me," Maxie whispered, a forever kind of love softening her eyes. "It's only fair that I rescue him back."

Things couldn't possibly get worse.

Connor was lying on a bunk in a jail cell in the Jackson Hole police station. For the first time in his life, he'd been arrested. Rocky Mountain Airlines had taken off into the wild blue yonder without him. Chagrined, he'd been forced to call Morris and beg him to drive to Jackson Hole and bail him out. That had been nearly six hours ago and there was still no sign of rescue.

On a more positive note, no one had strip-searched him.

He turned away a little metal tray bearing a wrinkled tuna sandwich and a bag of chips. His hangover was lingering stubbornly. The knuckles on his right hand were swollen to twice their normal size and throbbed like the devil. In addition, he had all the makings of a splendid black eye. He wondered disinterestedly if a black eye could be inflicted by falling on a roll of breath mints. Who knew? Who cared?

A commotion in the hallway raised a tiny flicker of hope. Perhaps this was Morris, at long last. Groaning, Connor rolled to his side and gingerly got to his feet, fighting a nauseating dizziness. He closed his eyes and counted to ten, willing his stomach to behave.

When he opened them, he forgot entirely about his wretched condition. Maxie Calhoon, live and in person, was walking down the hallway toward his cell, trailed by not one, not two, but no less than four deputies, each and every one wearing identical expressions of glassy-eyed bliss.

"You've all been so helpful," Maxie was saying, placing her hand over her heart. "What would I have done without you?"

"Our pleasure," chorused four voices.

Maxie stopped before Connor's cell, giving him a slow once-over from head to foot. "You look terrible," she pronounced. "And I hear you've been a bad boy."

"You look wonderful," Connor replied. She was wearing her jeans, boots and a blue denim shirt. No cowboy hat, no sunglasses to disguise her face. She seemed perfectly comfortable with several pairs of masculine eyes glued to her every movement.

"Morris and I had a little visit this morning," she said. "He told me you'd been arrested for disturbing the peace."

"I *was* disturbing the peace," Connor replied. He wanted to touch her in the worst way but there were several iron bars between them. "Maxie, seeing you is the best thing that's happened to me since the last time I saw you. But under the circumstances, visiting me in jail could result in even more publicity for you."

"I'm not visiting you," she said. "I'm your white knight who has come to rescue you. And I really don't give a damn about the publicity. Not anymore."

Connor opened his mouth and closed it again.

"Cat got your tongue?" Maxie asked, a sparkle in her eyes. "How unusual. I'll do the talking, then. I hear you quit your job."

"You heard right," Connor said, growing more confused by the minute.

"You enjoyed your job."

"I stopped enjoying it about four days ago."

She tilted her head thoughtfully, studying this man who had found his way into her heart in a few short days. His thick, caramel-colored hair was terribly mussed, sticking up this way and that. His poor, injured eye was a rainbow of blue, violet and yellow. His shirt was hanging out over his jeans and missing two buttons.

He was quite the most beautiful man she had ever met in her life, and definitely worth taking a chance for.

"What are you going to do now?" she asked.

"I haven't got a clue." Bewildered, Connor groped for words. "Maxie...why did you come?"

Violet eyes alight, she laughed softly. "Because you took me to a prom. Because you've never seen a lop-eared rabbit. Because you're my first love and I want you to be my last love."

The deputies froze, eyes riveted on the glorious woman declaring her love. This was Glitter Baby talking. They were witnessing history here.

"I'm sorry I didn't trust you before," she went on softly, her fingers curling around two of the metal bars. "I've learned to be so careful, but some things are worth taking a risk for. Yesterday, when you kept interrupting the interview, it seemed as if you weren't thinking about Glitter Baby at all, you were worried about Maxie Calhoon. Then when Morris told me who was responsible for the lien on the ranch, I realized how wrong I had been.'' She uncoiled a dazzling smile that cut to the very depths of him. "You aren't going to hurt me. I finally figured that out."

Connor touched his hand to hers, feeling the connection that went far beyond physical intimacy. His voice came softly, like a prayer. "Give me a lifetime to prove it to you. I love you, Maxie. I've loved you from the beginning. If you don't let me in your life…I don't know what will become of me." His eyes were hungry, touching on her hair, her skin, her lips. "We've only been apart for two days and I've already landed myself in jail. I'm lost without you, love."

Maxie's expression carried a heart-lifting sensuality. She sank against the bars, straining to get as close to him as possible. "I can face everything with you by my side. You give me a security I've never known. Forgive me for doubting you, Connor. I haven't had much experience with unconditional love."

There was so much expression on his face: tenderness, surprise, humility. "I never meant to hurt you, Maxie. I would move heaven and hell to keep you safe and happy."

A wicked smile curled her lips. "What else would you do, Connor? Hmmm?"

One of the deputies sat down abruptly on a nearby bench. He seemed to be hyperventilating.

"I'll tell you what, little girl. Get me out of here and I'll show you personally." He gave her a knowing smile, looking more and more like the cocky, confident man she had fallen in love with. "We'll retire to the closest hotel we can find. And we'll stay there until we've both gone blind from making mad, passionate, forever love.''

Another deputy whimpered and went down. You could hear a pin drop in the concrete hallway.

''All my life,'' Maxie whispered, ''there will be you, and only you. I want to have your babies. I want to watch sunsets with you. I want to wake up every morning and see you beside me. If you need to work in Los Angeles, I'll be right there with you. You're never going to shake me, Garrett. I have a habit of getting what I want.''

Connor himself was breathing a little irregularly. He wanted her lips, wanted that taste on his tongue. He wanted *out* of this damned jail cell.

''I don't like Los Angeles any more,'' he said. ''I'm in love with Oakley, Wyoming. I'd like to try my hand at writing and milking cows and working constantly on having babies...lots of babies.''

Maxie's hands were white-knuckled on the bars. Desire came to her like a flood, swirling around her heart and pooling in her secret places. Never once taking her eyes from Connor's, she said hoarsely, ''Officers? You need to let him out. Or let me in. I really don't care as long as I'm with him.''

Keys jangling, one of the deputies unlocked the cell. ''You're a lucky man,'' he muttered to Connor. ''*Real* lucky.''

The door swung open, and Connor and Maxie fell into each other's arms. They kissed, long, slow and deep. Neither of them cared who was watching or what they might think. When he reached the edges of his self-control, Connor pulled back, framing her face in his shaking hands. Oh, so beautiful, so sweet. Her violet eyes held nothing but him.

"Together," he whispered softly. "Always, from this day on."

The light in her eyes said yes.

Clearing their throats, the deputies shuffled down the corridor. To a man, they felt privileged. Even the circus of reporters and photographers gathered in the connecting office didn't mar their euphoria. They had seen Glitter Baby in love. Their fantasies would be particularly rich for some time to come.

Back in the hallway, still holding Maxie for all he was worth, Connor grinned. "You've just made four men very happy. No, make it five. You've made me ecstatic."

"I should warn you," Maxie ventured cautiously, "that you're bound to hear people talking about me, saying things you might not particularly like. You can't go around knocking them down all the time. One day the buzz will be over and the world will forget Glitter Baby ever existed. Until then, we'll just have to be patient. Yes?"

Connor nodded, looking at her as if he could taste her with his eyes. "Yes, dear. Whatever you say, dear."

Maxie's generous mouth tugged upwards in a sensual smile. "And you'll let me love you? Always and forever, with all my heart and body and soul?"

Every dream Connor had ever had in his life had come true in that moment. Tenderness filled him, warm, honeyed and incredibly powerful.

"Yes, dear," he whispered. "Oh, yes."

Some two hundred miles to the south, Jacob Stephens and Natalie Calhoon sat in a booth at Corner Drug, enjoying a banana split.

"So, do you think we should tell them?" Natalie asked.

Jacob feigned innocence. "Tell who what?"

Natalie's look said he wasn't fooling her for a minute. "Tell Connor and Maxie the truth."

"Oh, that." Jacob waved his spoon dismissively. "Why bother?"

Natalie chewed thoughtfully on her lower lip. "They might find out one day. They might feel…manipulated."

"We didn't do anything wrong," Jacob said firmly. "We met by accident when I wandered into your antique store two months ago. If we happened to talk about Connor and Maxie, if we decided they should meet, that's our business. They fell in love completely on their own."

"And the other?" Natalie persisted. "When they find out we've been seeing one another? Shouldn't we tell them?"

Jacob smiled tenderly. "They wouldn't believe us, anyway. We did too good a job of acting. Besides, I'm too short for you."

"And I'm too tall for you." She uttered a long, put-upon sigh. "What a shame. Oh, well. Would you like to see a movie tonight? Afterwards," she fluttered her lashes flirtatiously, "we could go back to my place and I'll show you my antiques."

*I'm a lucky man,* Jacob thought. This amazing woman had been well worth waiting for.

"Yes, dear," he said.

# Epilogue

There was only one photograph in the bedroom. It was small, but it occupied a place of honor on the wall opposite the bed. There were two people in the picture, both sun-bronzed, both smiling straight into the camera without a trace of pretense. They stood barefoot on a sandy beach, with a glorious backdrop of curling blue-and-white waves. There had been a wedding, obviously. The bride wore a simple white dress and carried a bouquet of tropical flowers. The breeze tousled her long hair like a lustrous garland. The groom had shunned a tuxedo for slacks and a loose white shirt, and someone had lovingly placed a lei around his neck. A rainbow-colored sunset poured over their happiness, gilding a precious moment in time.

"Are you awake?" Connor asked softly, his tender gaze moving from the photograph of his wife to the real thing beside him in the bed. When she didn't reply, he moved to the foot of the bed and sat cross-legged on the tumbled sheets, staring at her while she enjoyed another three minutes of sleep. Then, a bit louder this time: "Maxie? Are you awake?"

"Uh-uh." Her face was half buried in the pillow, muffling her voice. "Sleeping..."

Connor grinned, knowing all too well the reason for his beloved's exhaustion. "Honey Bun? Snookums? Wake up, this is really important."

Maxie sighed deeply, turning over on her back. Her face was sleep-flushed, her eyelids heavy and her luscious mouth drowsy. This, Connor thought with a hot rush of passion, was definitely a picture he needed to capture on film. Maxie Garrett in bed and in love. She put the rest of the world to shame without even trying.

"I have something very important to ask you," he whispered, devouring her with his eyes. "Are you awake?"

"Let me think." She stretched both arms above her head, sending the white bedsheet to an indecent level beneath her rose-tipped breasts. She loved to look at him in the mornings, with his thick hair tangled and his skin marked with the flush of sleep. It reminded her of the way he looked when they made love, so hot and wild, his glittering eyes intense with a never-sated need. "Maybe. Probably. I love you, Connor."

"I love you back." His eyes softened with a smile that came from his heart. He was all too conscious of the trust this woman had placed in him. He could never do enough for her, never love her enough to repay her for what she had given him. Faith. Happiness. Sunlight. Love that doubled and redoubled every moment they spent together. How had he lived so long without this? They were a family now, just the two of them. Whatever life had in store for them, they would meet together. "I just realized something. I don't know what color our children's hair will be."

"Our children's hair?" Maxie echoed, her dreamy gaze focusing on his narrow hips. Sadly, rumpled satin sheets obstructed a complete view. Her imagination kicked in and a flame flickered to life deep in her belly. "You've lost me."

"Never," Connor promised softly. "Still, here we are married and all and I don't know what color your hair is. When you modeled, it was a dark gold. Now it's auburn. Both look wonderful on you, but then again, green hair would look wonderful on you. So which is it?"

"I went lighter when I modeled," Maxie said through a drowsy yawn, "but I had a brunette past. I went back to my roots, so to speak. Now you know all my womanly secrets."

She had no idea how staggering her beauty was, her violet eyes gleaming with a soft invitation, a dusky curl clinging to her throat in a teasing question mark. Just looking at her—his *wife,* he thought with silent amazement—made him crazy with need. "So our girls will be dark-headed angels, just like you."

"And the boys," Maxie murmured, "will be dazzling charmers like their father. Unless heaven throws us a curve. It happens sometimes, you know." Her hips began to move restlessly, sending the white sheet to her waist. "How many do you want?"

Connor was watching the seductive movements of her lithe body, his mouth suddenly dry. "How many what?"

"Children." Bold in her new role as experienced wife, Maxie caught her bottom lip between her teeth, gently caressing his chest with soft fingers. She loved the hectic fire that flashed into Connor's eyes. In her humble opinion, she had a gift for the powerful sexual secrets Connor had so tenderly revealed to her. "Would you like more than two?"

"Two what?" There seemed to be a lack of oxygen in the room. "Maxie, you're killing me. My self-control only goes—"

"I'd like four," she interrupted serenely. Her fingers continued their erotic exploration, a new wildness heating her from inside. "Uhmmm...this feels good. You know what?"

"Dear heaven." He closed his eyes briefly. "What?"

"I'm hungry."

*"Hungry?"*

She nodded, the tip of her tongue touching the corner of her mouth. "Not for food, poor man. I don't care if I never have another can of SpaghettiOs. We're going to live on love. Morning, noon, night, week after week, month after month." She smiled ever so slowly, crooking a beckoning finger.

Connor's eyes narrowed, his pulse coming hard and fast in his throat. "Don't make promises you can't keep, baby. I'll hold you to them."

"Come here," she whispered. "I need to kiss you."

Instead of obeying her, Connor caught the white sheet half-heartedly covering her and pulled it slowly towards him. Each revealing inch gave him another view to treasure: the pearly skin of her breasts topped with pink rosebuds, her flat stomach, the soft honey-colored hair at the juncture of her thighs. "Sweetheart, you are so…"

Maxie pressed a frustrated fist to her mouth, her skin tingling from the slow movement of the cool satin sheet. "I'm so what?"

"Precious," he said simply, tiring of the game. He stretched out against her in a rush, catching her hands in his and holding them above her head. He was already hard and Maxie gasped as she felt his warmth between her legs.

"Now you've got me," she managed, "what are you going to do with me?"

Connor kissed her, anointing her throat, then moving to the baby-soft, responsive lips. "It would be easier," he murmured, "to tell you what I'm *not* going to do to you."

Maxie was squirming. She loved his open-mouthed kisses, his experienced tongue…and oh, when he released her hands and trailed his pleasure-giving mouth lower…this sent scalding ribbons of sensation through her hot body. Her excitement grew in intensity as she tried to prolong the exquisite rapture. "I love…*oh*…"

Connor smiled shakily against her perfumed skin. "You love this?"

Her hands tangled in his hair. "I love you. And this…"

"And this…?" Connor's pulse was off the charts. His skin glistened hotly as he became wild, losing control in that way he had that made her body desperate with need. "And this…"

*"Everything."* Maxie loved this side of him, when he became gloriously, elementally male. His hard-boned body, erotic mouth and seeking hands all adored her body, weighting her limbs and obliterating her thoughts like a powerful drug. Knowing she could make him lose control was an added aphrodisiac. She arched hard against him, deliberately adding fuel to the fire. Her fingers dug into his back as she felt the urgent pressure between her legs. Raw hunger, desperation, exhilaration...she felt it all swirling through her bloodstream like a powerful, forbidden drug.

Connor lifted his head, staring down into her flushed face with heavy-lidded golden eyes. "Look at me," he whispered. "Look in my eyes when I..." He groaned involuntarily as he entered her. Then, when her mouth parted and her eyes drifted closed to savor the sensation, he shook her shoulders. *"No.* Look at me. Feel it with me. Stay with me while we go out of our minds, Maxie..."

And stay with him she did. She held his eyes when he increased his movements, clung to them as she spiralled higher and cried out for release. Never once, never once did they break that contact that went soul-deep.

Connor's thoughts were a restless, reckless blur. He bit his lips as he drove deeper within her. He tasted a drop of blood, his breath coming in hard, racking shivers. And through it all he drifted in her eyes. In their loving, violet depths he saw the man he hoped to become. When she looked at him like that, he knew he could move mountains for her. And he would if she asked it of him.

"Now..." Maxie was trembling, moist with sexual heat. She felt him lifting her hips with his hands, giving him deeper access. Hard, fast…he took her to the edge of sanity with his fevered rhythm. Never once did he look away. And when their muscles tensed in a delirium of passion, she held fiercely to his eyes. They clung together as they reached the summit, held tightly as the frantic, pleasure-shudders spread like a sea of fireworks deep in their bodies. Together, intertwined in body and mind, they had made a pilgrimage. And together they'd found their miracle—the sweet understanding of longing and the eternal prospect of fulfillment.

Afterwards they lay together in weary, soft-fleshed bliss. Connor was stroking Maxie's damp hair, his eyes focused on her moist, kiss-stung lips. At times, she seemed much older than her tender years, but now he saw her youth, so pure and hopeful it wrenched his heart.

"To see you," he whispered huskily, "is to love you. I knew that from the beginning. You're my love, my best friend, my wife…everything I need on God's green earth I found in you."

She smiled tremulously, her eyes bright as sequins. "Tell me, Connor, do you feel married?"

His answer was soft, and straight from his heart. "Since the first day I saw you, angel. Since the very first day."

"Connor?"

He nuzzled her throat. "Yes?"

"I'm hungry."

His head came up. "Maxie, I'm only human. We just—"

"Not for *that*," she chastised, her smile teasing.

"For food. Then I'll have enough energy for the other kind of hunger. How about waffles? With big, luscious strawberries and mounds of lovely whipped cream."

"Whipped cream?" Now she had his attention. "Mounds of it?"

"Oodles," she promised.

"Can we have this breakfast in bed?"

Maxie might have been fairly new at physical intimacy, but she was nobody's fool. Eyes sparkling, she ruffled the top of his head. "Silly man. I'm way, *way* ahead of you."

\* \* \* \* \*

# *Desire celebrates Silhouette's 20th anniversary in grand style!*

## Don't miss:

- ### *The Dakota Man* by Joan Hohl
  Another unforgettable MAN OF THE MONTH
  On sale October 2000

- ### *Marriage Prey* by Annette Broadrick
  Her special anniversary title!
  On sale November 2000

- ### *Slow Fever* by Cait London
  Part of her new miniseries FREEDOM VALLEY
  On sale December 2000

## Plus:

### FORTUNE'S CHILDREN: THE GROOMS
On sale August through December 2000
Exciting new titles from Leanne Banks, Kathryn Jensen,
Shawna Delacorte, Caroline Cross and Peggy Moreland

Every woman wants to be loved...
### BODY & SOUL
Desire's highly sensuous new promotion features stories
from Jennifer Greene, Anne Marie Winston
and Dixie Browning!

*Available at your favorite retail outlet.*

*Where love comes alive™*

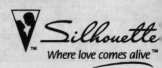

Coming Soon
Silhouette Books presents

*Weddings in White*

(on sale September 2000)

A 3-in-1 keepsake collection
by international bestselling author

# DIANA PALMER

Three heart-stoppingly handsome bachelors are paired
up with three innocent beauties who long to marry the
men of their dreams. This dazzling collection showcases
the enchanting characters and searing passion that
has made Diana Palmer a legendary talent
in the romance industry.

*Unlikely Lover:*
Can a feisty secretary and a gruff oilman fight
the true course of love?

*The Princess Bride:*
For better, for worse, starry-eyed Tiffany Blair captivated
Kingman Marshall's iron-clad heart....

*Callaghan's Bride:*
Callaghan Hart swore marriage was for fools—until
Tess Brady branded him with her sweetly seductive kisses!

*Available at your favorite retail outlet.*

*Silhouette*®
*Where love comes alive*™

Visit Silhouette at www.eHarlequin.com          PSWIW

# COMING NEXT MONTH

**#1321 THE DAKOTA MAN—Joan Hohl**

*Man of the Month*

Mitch Grainger always got what he wanted…and what he wanted was his new assistant, Maggie Reynolds. The cunning businessman decided to make Maggie his reward in the ultimate game of seduction…never dreaming *his* heart might become *her* pawn.

**#1322 RANCHER'S PROPOSITION—Anne Marie Winston**

*Body & Soul*

All he wanted was a woman to share his ranch—not his bed. But when Lyn Hamill came to work on Cal McCall's South Dakota spread, he began to rethink his intentions. And though Lyn's eyes spoke of a dark past, Cal was determined to make her his wife in every way....

**#1323 FIRST COMES LOVE—Elizabeth Bevarly**

She'd had a crush on him since she was seven. But it wasn't until her entire hometown suspected Tess Monahan was pregnant that Will Darrow suddenly started showing up at her house offering a helping hand. Now if she could only convince him that she didn't want his hand but his heart....

**#1324 FORTUNE'S SECRET CHILD—Shawna Delacorte**

*Fortune's Children: The Grooms*

He thought he would never see Cynthia McCree again. Then suddenly she was back in town—and back in Shane Fortune's life. He had never stopped caring for the vulnerable beauty, but once he discovered the truth about her past, would he still want to make her his Fortune bride?

**#1325 MAROONED WITH A MARINE—Maureen Child**

*Bachelor Battalion*

One hurricane, one motel room—and one very sexy Marine—added up to trouble for Karen Beckett. She knew that Gunnery Sergeant Sam Paretti wouldn't leave her alone in the storm. But how did she convince him to stay once the danger had passed…?

**#1326 BABY: MacALLISTER-MADE—Joan Elliott Pickart**

*The Baby Bet*

They had one passionate night together, one that best friends Brenda Henderson and Richard MacAllister knew should never be repeated. Then Brenda announced she was pregnant. Now Richard had to convince Brenda that his proposal of marriage was not based on duty…but on love.

CMN0900